FRIENDS | NEVER KNEW

Dear Annette,
I really
value your
stories and
conversation.

TANYA LESTER

Tanya Lester

gynergy books

ACKNOWLEDGEMENTS

The author wishes to thank the Manitoba Arts Council
for its financial assistance.

Part of this book was developed at the Delta Marsh
Writers' Retreat, sponsored by the Manitoba Writers'
Guild.

"Lady Slipper," pp. 153-154, was originally published
in Contemporary Verse 2, March 1992.

Thanks to Lillian Allen for kind permission to quote
from her work (p.144). From *Revolutionary Tea
Party*, Verse to Vinyl, 1985.

The publisher thanks the Canada Council for its kind support.

Edited by Lynn Henry
Cover Art, *Mandala in Remembrance of Summer*, by
Heidi Eigenkind
Cover and book design by Catherine Matthews
Printed and bound in Canada by
Imprimerie d'Éditions Marquis Ltée

for

gynergy books
P.O. Box 2023
Charlottetown, Prince Edward Island
Canada C1A 7N7

Canadian Cataloguing in Publication Data

Lester, Tanya, 1956-
Friends I never knew
ISBN 0-921881-18-5

I. Title.
PS8573.E746F75 1992   C813'.54   C92-098534-3
PR9199.3.L57F75 1992

To the Manitoba Action Committee on the Status of Women, and to all the friends I know who are writing their life stories.

CONTENTS

TARA   7

JUANITA   11

TARA   39

LOU   43

TARA   71

MIRIAM   73

TARA   89

RITA   93

TARA   111

JUANITA   113

TARA   147

TARA'S STORY
(a fragment)   151

TARA   157

TARA

We are in a circle, the five of us around an open fire in a field in a leftover world. Everything is grey—our robes, the shawls that cover our heads, the grass, the tumbleweeds, the sky, the earth. Only the horizon far away in the distance is a thread of yellow. And the fire, of course, but even its flames are muted orange and yellow. All of us are bleeding. Burgundy clots of blood seep through the bodices of our robes.

The women move but not to stop the bleeding. Lou, who is already talking, lies down on her side as she continues. Miriam moves over to cradle the older woman's head in her lap and begins to speak herself. Rita stands up and shouts defiantly. Juanita gathers stones and begins shaping them into a woman's body as she chats like she does when drinking tea with a friend.

I say nothing, do nothing, but I hear their voices. No one else does.

And we go on bleeding.

I wake up to the sweet—almost rotten—smell of flowers and know immediately that I am no longer in Winnipeg where the nightmare first visited me. I am in Cyprus. My hands move over to the other side of the bed. The sheets are crumpled but he is gone.

It's since I moved to this island half way around the world from home that those women haunt my thoughts. Walking along the harbour at sunset, I see someone who looks so much like Miriam I call out her name before I realize my mistake in the puzzled eyes of a woman who turns at the sound of my voice.

Plucking mandarin oranges off a tree by the caves, I hold one up to my nose and the fragrance is Juanita, who would pass me her blue clay bowl filled with the same kind of fruit. From my balcony, one day leads into another and another with no end to the old women who hobble by with spirits bent, until I wake up one night terrified to see the ghost of my old age looming ahead of me. It is Lou who rescues me, as I remember the pride with which she carried her ancient being. And so it is with Miriam and Rita and others, too. Love and wonder and caring and hurt, I feel for them.

Their talk of their lives was like a gift. In the notebook I kept in the side drawer of my office desk in Winnipeg I would scribble fragments, expressions, sketchy descriptions of what each looked like, key phrases from their storytelling. Anything to make me remember those stories later on.

But back then, when they told their stories, my vision was blurred by my work for a feminist group. I lived twenty-four hours a day for the movement. Even at night, I would lie awake on my pillow planning a protest demonstration or an annual general meeting or what I might say to the media at a press conference.

It was like I was caught in a trap. I was obsessed with making things better for women. A letter and telegram campaign to persuade the prime minister to include a women's equal status clause in the Canadian constitution would be followed by an election. Then, I would plunge into the coordination of women's delegations to visit prospective MPs during the election campaign. It went on and on like this. Some women drop friends for marriage and raising kids. I dropped friends for the women's movement.

Now I realize that it was not only my strong desire to fight against sexism that kept me going but those women and their stories, too. They filled me, gave my life a sense of complete roundness. It was their stories, bits and pieces of their experiences, I chose to keep in my green notebook for the future.

I get up, put on my bathrobe, turn on the light and sit down in front of my typewriter. I see through the sliding windows of my balcony the outlines of the Greek Orthodox Church, its rounded stone roof, the flat tops of the restaurants and shops. The sea water, down by the harbour, glistens as it slaps in tiny waves under the moonlight. At the horizon, there is a thread of yellow light.

I roll a blank piece of paper into the typewriter.

JUANITA

I met Juanita soon after I agreed to represent my employer, Women for Equality, as chairperson of the International Women's Day Committee. The committee was a coalition of women's groups with a mandate to organize events and celebrations on and around International Women's Day. In Winnipeg, as in several other cities across Canada, the IWD Committee was a hotbed of clashing political ideologies. Besides several immigrant and ethnic women's groups, the Committee attracted Communist Party members, Trotskyites, a smattering of liberals, lesbian separatists, feminists from the left, right and centre with as many sexual preferences, and a few non-aligned but bewildered individuals. As chair, I often felt like a referee in a boxing ring. Women spat insults at each other across the bingo hall tables at our weekly meetings in the Women for Equality office. This is not to say that the end result—the rallies, speeches, table displays, workshops and musical entertainment—was anything less than a joyful celebration of our sisterhood. But my year on the IWD Committee was one entwined with exhilaration and frustration.

From my vantage point at the head of the table, I soon became curious about Juanita because she never embroiled herself in the debate that ricocheted around the room. She stood out in other ways, too. She didn't quite fit in with the other Latin American women she accompanied to and from the meetings. Sure, she was the only one among them from Guatemala, but it was more than that. It was the way she dressed in blue jeans and shirt tails or a sweatshirt, usually red, while the others tended to wear dresses. Her dark hair fell in unruly waves almost to her shoulders and a bright scarf was often tied around the top of her head, while the others had hair cut modestly and manageably short. Her face was plain with rather thick eyebrows hanging over dark brown eyes, but under her calm surface I could detect a vitality that sometimes painted her cheeks red. Once, this happened when her Latin American sisters were vehemently arguing against any discussion of abortion among presentations for IWD. I guessed (correctly, as I later found out) that she had no quarrel with the principles of reproductive choice although she, like the others, had been raised on the Roman Catholic doctrine. The other thing that made her stand out was her size. She was the shortest among those who attended our weekly Wednesday night meeting, although her somewhat stocky build suggested strength. I put some of her difference down to age. Juanita, in her thirties, was ten to fifteen years younger than the others.

It took several meetings before it became apparent to me that the others had persuaded her to sit on the Committee because she was an artist, and willing to design posters to publicize the IWD events at no cost.

It was her poster design that lead me to Juanita's apartment one evening. I had agreed to pick up the design and take it to the printer the following day. It was five o'clock in early December, and already quite dim as I stood in the hallway of Juanita's apartment, waiting for her to bring me the artwork. As my eyes grew accustomed to the dark I couldn't pull them away from the ink drawings pinned to one side of the coat closet.

They were sketches of women giving birth. One woman, her hands squeezed around an intricately designed bedpost, was squatting with her back arched away from her wooden support as the baby's head crowned between her legs. The legs were patterned with what seemed like hundreds of muscles and were as wonderfully detailed as the bedpost.

The other drawing was of an enormous woman who stood with her legs parted wide in a warrior position, hands clutched to a belly which rolled into the smaller hills in the background. From between her legs gushed a stream of breaking waters.

When my eyes moved up, I saw a face unmasked by pain. If one looked long enough, I felt, it would be possible to become familiar with the intimate details of that woman's life.

"Would you wish to see more?"

I started, and turned to find Juanita standing behind me with a beige folder containing the poster artwork in one hand.

"Yes ... Yes, I would," I said, as I awkwardly jammed the folder into my handbag.

"Come then," she said, and motioned me to follow her into a room up the hall and to the left, from which a beam of electric light shone.

I quickly pulled off my boots and padded after her on the hardwood floor. The room turned out to be a narrow kitchen occupied by a young woman who looked to be about fifteen. With a fork in one hand, she stirred a pan filled with zucchini, while her other hand rested on the lid of a pot in which something was boiling. Under her chin she cradled a phone receiver. Juanita turned down the stove in passing and gently but firmly steered the young woman to one side so we could pass through the doorway at the other end of the kitchen.

"... and then Jacques pushed me against the wall and I said, 'What is it that you think you are doing? You have no right to ... ' "

As we moved into the next room I could no longer hear the young woman's chatter. Here, in the sitting room, two boys of maybe ten and twelve years were squabbling in Spanish as the older one switched the television from one channel to another. The television provided the only light in the room.

The squabbling brought a well-groomed man out of an adjacent bedroom, but not before he had switched on a light in the bedroom, exposing a baby in a crib. The man admonished the boys in Spanish. After the boys had stopped yelling, Juanita introduced the man to me as her husband, Rodriguez. His palm was rough but warm when we shook hands.

"Come," Juanita told me again. We crossed the sitting room and entered a smaller space. It was a balcony-porch and had plastic stapled over its row of windows.

Juanita pulled the cord from an overhead light bulb and there they were. Women. All of them in childbirth. Twisting, pushing, heaving. Babies' heads and shoulders entering the outside from between flabby legs, scrawny legs, hairy legs. Babies in arms or suckling breasts. A baby born still. A woman too exhausted to weep. There were bloody afterbirths and cords and soiled sheets. There were women in beds or crouched on the floor. One was in a cart driven by a donkey. Another was in a dry bathtub.

The artwork was a mixture of oil paintings, pastels, ink or charcoal drawings and pencil sketches. They were propped up on a blue enamel table and pinned to the grey walls above the windows. Some sat on different-sized easels and others were hung on a line from the ceiling.

Without thinking, I pulled a chair out from the table and sat down. It was too much beauty in one place. The smell of paint tickled my nose.

Juanita put her hand against a teapot on the part of the table not cluttered with pictures and art materials. "It is still very warm," she said. "Would you like a cup?"

"Yes, please."

Next to the pot was a blue bowl full of mandarin oranges. "Here," she said and pushed it towards me.

She left me for a moment and returned with a chipped teacup. "I am sorry all the others are not washed," she said, and poured tea into that cup and another already sitting on the table.

"Don't worry about it," I said, and waved my hand at the pictures. "They're all of women giving birth."

Juanita smiled at my stating the obvious. "Yes, I am a midwife of twenty-five years now. It is from this work that the paintings come."

"But you don't seem old enough to have twenty-five years' experience in midwifery."

"When you start as a young girl, you become old in experience before your years."

"And the art?"

"I began to draw from the first time I saw a woman give birth."

After I had asked a few more questions, Juanita must have

realized I was sincerely interested. I think she was also yearning to talk to someone about her past in Guatemala. She sat down at the table, knotted her hands around her warm cup of tea and opened herself to me. It was long after her daughter had called her to supper and long after she had shouted back a "momento" and rose to close the door to the balcony porch, that she finished telling me the first of what turned out to be many stories from her past.

As we sat in that artwork-filled room, Juanita told me that she had first assisted in birth when she was ten years old—one third of my age. Her cousin Julie went into labour when Juanita's mother, who was the village midwife, was away at the town market selling her vegetables. But there was no stopping that baby, who was determined to get out into the world.

Juanita had watched Julie slowly make her way from her home on the hill down towards the village. Ribbons of gold, red and aqua-blue streamed from Julie's hair. Her body, which was close to bursting, was clothed in a heavy cotton dress of red and yellow stripes that is the traditional garb of the Guatemalan people. Down the path she came, through the green onions grown by Juanita's father on the steppes his grandfather had cut out of the hills a century before. Once in awhile she would stop and sway with labour pains.

Soon, when Julie was among the chickens that Juanita hated so much, with their shitty yellow markings in their green and copper-brown feathers, Juanita ran to meet Julie and guided the pregnant woman to the safety of their home. It would be terrible, she thought, to allow Julie to stand among those clucking vultures with the baby about to come.

Even today when Juanita smells chicken shit on a farm in the countryside, it reminds her of her family's poverty. As a child she would dream of murdering those chickens in a splendid flash of axes. But no—her mother had to keep them for extra income. So she never felt truly free when running home from school in the afternoon or coming down from work in the hills in the evening because ahead of her was the task of feeding those cackling creatures. Later, her art teacher would show her oil paintings of those birds and tell her about Chagall's paintings. They could keep their chickens, Juanita thought. Chagall, she was sure, had never scratched his body as it jumped with their fleas and lice.

In fact, on the day before Julie descended the hill, the rooster had taken a flying leap at Juanita. She showed me the scar still there on her neck.

Upon hearing her eldest child's screams Juanita's mother had run out of the house and, grabbing a machete, had caught that rooster by its legs, placed her foot on its neck and cut its head off. She had plucked its feathers right there and gutted it, before Juanita's father could get home to yell at her. Next day she took that rooster to the market to sell alongside her vegetables, and in the evening she returned with its replacement.

By the time that particular evening came, however, Juanita had nothing else on her mind except the baby girl her cousin had birthed with her help. And from that day on, Juanita believed that life follows death, and that good comes to take the place of evil. She carried this belief in her heart in later years when she went to work for the revolution, and it kept her going.

On the afternoon we are talking about, though, nothing mattered except Julie's contractions, which were coming closer and closer together and with increasing force. Juanita put Julie on her own cot and built up the fire in the middle of the dirt floor in the kitchen. She was already sweating from the heat, but it was the only thing she could think of doing to avoid the eyes of her grandmother, who sat in the corner of the room, clothed in black from head to foot. Juanita was in awe of her grandmother, who had assisted at many births.

The grandmother's hands, experienced with guiding so many little heads out of birth canals, lay gnarled and useless in her lap. They were too stiff now for the job. Her daughter, Juanita's mother, whom the old woman had trained to carry on her work, would not be back for hours. Both grandmother and granddaughter knew this.

"Juanita, you must listen and I will tell you what to do," the old woman said quietly. Juanita wanted to run away, to jump up right then and hide away like a scared rabbit. She was filled with terror.

Her hands shook as she found one of her mother's nightgowns for Julie. Before she helped her cousin put it on, Juanita held it to her nose and breathed deeply of its fresh smell, which came from drying on a rock near the lake. It was good, but not enough to stop her from shaking.

For the next several hours, her cousin could not sit still nor stop herself from screaming. Juanita brought Julie water, massaged her back with little, clammy cold hands, and looked to her grandmother for guidance. Surely, Juanita thought, her grandmother would come up with something to stop the pain. By the end of the day, she knew different.

"Stay near to catch the baby when it journeys out," the grandmother said, from where she stood at the open door to keep Juanita's younger brothers and sisters outside. "It will come through between her legs and it will not be long now."

Juanita thought to herself, "I must not let the baby drop." She scurried around after Julie with her hands out in front of her. At first her cousin was kneeling on the floor. Then she would move back onto the bed or stand up or pace up and down the kitchen. Juanita followed her, arms stretched out, hands cupped together. She felt as horrible as one of those chickens. She could hear her grandmother laughing softly.

Then, the miracle happened. Juanita saw the baby's head begin to slide out of the mother. At first, she forgot to get under Julie to hold onto the baby. She crossed herself instead. Later, she felt silly about that, too.

She did catch the baby in the end and she wondered at its slippery little body, smeared with blood and slime. She wondered at its beauty. Then Julie began to laugh, and Juanita joined in, and soon her grandmother laughed too. The old woman's face became smooth, and her hands worked again for as long as it took to cut the cord and tie it with a small piece of rope. Next she sent Juanita to bring in the basin from under the outside pump. When Juanita rushed inside with it, she saw her grandmother rub and rub Julie's belly until a big red sponge of blood spilled out.

With that done, both Julie and her grandmother sank back in exhaustion while Juanita busied herself with the chores of throwing away the afterbirth and cleaning the baby. Soon the house was full again, with Julie's husband and the children. Juanita's father, and then her mother, returned from work.

Juanita was allowed a rest from helping her mother make the tacos for the evening meal, while her grandmother told the family about how Juanita was becoming a midwife so soon, at the age of ten. Juanita's mother could not contain her pride and seemed, to Juanita, puffed out and round with pleasure. She seemed almost as pleased as Julie, who held her baby, wrapped in white linen, close to her body.

By nightfall Juanita was exhausted, but she could not sleep until she did something with the images from the day still clear in her head. With a lit candle, she found a pencil and a paper from her school things. She drew the baby girl surfacing from her mother, and more pictures of Julie, and so on and on. Finally, she had drawn all the images out of herself and slept a deep, deep sleep. Her work was done.

Juanita's mistake was leaving those drawings out, next to where she slept under her blanket on the dirt floor. In the early morning her father spied them and she woke to the noise of his shouting.

" Throw them in the fire," he yelled. " They are dirty. What you have there is dirty." He dragged Juanita up from the floor, yanked at her arm until she found her feet and thrust the pictures into her hand.

Her mother sat poking at the fire she had just built. She looked so small to her daughter now, and the roundness from the day before seemed like nothing more than drooping flesh. She looked at her feet and not into Juanita's face.

Juanita said nothing. She burned the pictures, crumpled them into a ball and burned them. Later, she drew them again and this time she hid them. Each time she finished helping at a birth after that, she drew what she saw. For years she believed she was like one of the saints of old who had been persecuted and forced to hide.

When she told me this story on that first occasion, sitting in her balcony-porch, she thought her idea about the saints was very funny. She felt much more powerful now. God and her father no longer ruled her, and her sense of the beauty of birth was even stronger than it had been back then.

Juanita's story freed something in me. Even on that first night, what Juanita had told me cleared away the jumbled thoughts I usually had after going to bed. I was open, clean, as one feels after a long hot bath. I did not work out exactly what I was going to say at next day's press conference on Equal Pay for Work of Equal Value. I didn't even think about all the women I had to phone in order to get the Violence Against Women Committee off the ground. I put off all this head-work until the next day. I fell into an easy sleep.

I found out more about Juanita when we were working on a mailout of hundreds of invitations to the IWD celebration. I remember it was later that evening, after the canvas bags were tied and ready to be taken down to the main post office in the morning, that I stayed in the office to begin jotting down parts of her story.

I had bought the green notebook on the way to work earlier in the day, and intended to use it to keep an itemized account of the office expenses. Instead, it became a log book, and Juanita's stories were the first entries. All of a sudden, the reason for jotting down these women's stories had became personal as well as political.

That afternoon and evening as we worked, Juanita told me about the beauty of her home town, San Pedro. She described its location, on a lake surrounded by volcanoes. The clouds there seemed to cling to the mountaintops as if making love to them. Juanita would go up into the hills to pick onions—not something that she found very romantic. But when she looked down into the valley and over the lake, she saw magnificence.

In her paintings there was always some symbol of her home if you looked carefully and knew what to look for. Perhaps there would be a woman giving birth in a bedroom or on a narrow hospital bed. Juanita would be true to the woman's posture, but would rest the woman's body on the edge of clear Lake Atitlan. Or the outlines of a mountain could be traced on the woman's abdomen and pubic mound, as if the artwork was from the point of view of someone looking down on her body from over her shoulder. Juanita told the women stories of her homeland to pass the time if the labour was long, so the sketches of her homeland meshed very naturally with sketches of women giving birth.

Juanita did have some art school training. She came to attend the school through her mother, who was selling vegetables in the market and happened to be in the right place at the right time.

Juanita's mother knew about her daughter's drawings, and liked them. She helped hide them from Juanita's father by placing them in her daughter's hope chest. One day she came back from the market and Juanita had never seen her so happy. Her cheeks were bright red and even when the children misbehaved, she only laughed. She had brought candy back with her and instead of spanking her youngest when he begged, she gave him more.

Juanita's father was the first one to go to sleep after the evening meal. When he was out of the way, she called her eldest daughter close and whispered the story of her day so that the other children would not hear. She said that a special man had visited the market that day. He had talked to Juanita's uncle, her mother's brother, who sold his pottery there.

The man was an artist from the United States and had lived in a nearby village for years, producing his paintings. Now he had been hired by the United Nations to find Guatemalans with artistic potential and help teach them, to encourage them to paint from their surroundings and culture. Juanita's uncle explained all this to Juanita's mother, who was excited by the news. She told her brother to tell the artist about Juanita's pictures.

The artist sent word back that he wanted to see the girl's

work, and he asked if her mother could bring some of Juanita's pictures to the market on the following day. If she could, he would drop by and take a look. Juanita is sure he did not expect much, and probably thought her mother might not even bother to bring the pictures. But then, the man did not know Juanita's mother. She took his request very seriously.

In fact, Juanita's mother decided that Juanita should be there to present her work. So she prepared her daughter for the event. She brought out Juanita's best navy school tunic and whitest blouse, the ones she wore only on special days. She boiled water in the huge rusty pot that hung over the fire just outside the front door and gave her daughter a bath, even though Juanita had been keeping herself clean for years already. Then, she worked late into the night to make sure the vegetables would be clean and beautiful for the next day.

In the morning, she told her daughter to set off for school as usual, but then to wait on the road for her mother. Juanita asked no questions. She knew if her father found out about their plans, it would not be good for her or her mother. As for the pictures, Juanita's mother said she was to take all of them.

At the market, they waited and waited and waited. They began to worry that the artist had forgotten them. But a little before noon, he came. Juanita had never seen a gringo up close before. Now one was smiling at her and shaking her hand. Her mother gave him a bundle of vegetables before he had the chance to look at the pictures. The artist said it was not necessary. He grew his own garden and this was his job, to look at the pictures. But Juanita's mother, shy in public on most occasions, insisted. Never before had Juanita seen her mother so forward with a man. Then the artist spoke in Spanish to her mother. Juanita wondered why he had not spoken to her like this from the beginning.

She thought about these things later. At the time, she was too busy trembling. She thought she would die of fright as he fingered through her crude little drawings. Finally, he stopped nodding and asked her mother how old Juanita was. She was fourteen, her mother told him, in her last year at school. The artist said that, for a girl so young, her work was very fine. Very fine. Those words seemed, to Juanita, the best ever invented. She said she would never forget how he looked, how her mother looked, how her uncle looked when he said those words. Very fine. Then he talked to her uncle in English and turned to shake her hand. If nothing more than that had happened, Juanita was sure she would have walked with her feet barely touching the earth for many, many days.

But after the artist had left, Juanita's uncle told them that the artist would be setting up a summer school in his village. He wondered if there was a way for Juanita to attend. Of course there was! Juanita's cousin lived in the artist's village. It was settled, then. Word came that the artist would expect Juanita to be at his school on June 24 at nine in the morning—the date and time were indelible in Juanita's memory. From that moment on her life would never be the same.

On the morning she was to leave by bus, her mother gave Juanita a bundle of clothes newly clean from the pounding she had given them by the lake the day before. She gave her daughter some money that she had set aside from selling vegetables, to pay the driver, and two live chickens for their cousin. Another small bundle contained some tacos spread with jam and a single boiled egg for lunch.

With Juanita's bundles set on the outside of the doorway, her father was told of her plans. He said no, and began to shout. Juanita's mother told her daughter to run for the bus as fast as she could. It was difficult to run with the cage of chickens and bundles but Juanita was determined to get away. Her father, it turned out, would have to do without her for the coffee tree tending that summer. Juanita left, though, to the sounds of her father beating her mother. It seemed to Juanita that he was beating her harder than he had ever beat her before.

On the bus, she closed her eyes tight and thought only of the artist's smile. It kept her going. Worry for her mother and fear of the drunk man who was sitting next to her would have overcome her if she had not had the artist to think about. Although she was fourteen, this was only the second time she had been on a bus in her entire life.

Juanita worked hard that summer. She had always worked hard in her short lifetime—picking coffee and vegetables, feeding animals, looking out for the children, helping at births, washing clothes and helping her mother prepare meals. But she worked just as hard, in a way, that summer. She would go to school all day and then tend to the supper and watch her cousin's children at night. There was no question that she would help her cousin, who had small children, in any way possible, as thanks for staying there at no charge.

Still, she never felt tired. Each day there was something new. She learned to paint her drawings and then the fields and the workers. Some days they painted in the golden cathedral and the artist would talk about it being such a shame to see all this gold when people outside were begging. So his students painted the beggars, too. Then the artist gave the beggars some coins, saying that they had to eat and it was not right for artists to exploit their poverty. Later, Juanita thought it would have been better to at least ask the beggars if they felt it was alright to be subjects for painting, to allow them the dignity of saying yes or no.

The beggar Juanita painted was out in front of the cathedral whenever Juanita passed by or came to paint with the others. The old woman wore clothes of brown cotton, draped over head and body. Juanita thought the clothes had probably been another colour—bright red, or blue and gold, maybe—when the woman had danced through life in her youth. When Juanita knew her, however, she did no dancing. The best she could do was crawl for coins tossed out of her reach. She used one knee, for the other leg was cut off above where the knee had been. The flies, who fed in her open sores, were her constant and only companions. Sometimes as she sat a few feet away with her canvas on its easel, Juanita would try to talk to the woman. Never did the beggar answer. Either she could not hear or would not hear, her mind having long ago left the pain of her body, except for the small part that remained to care for her basic needs.

But usually Juanita's thoughts were not so very deep. There

was, after all, the artist—or Señor Forest, for that was his name. Juanita's dark thoughts would vanish when she thought of him. Even when he insisted each day that she and the others should do some regular school work—maths, science and the languages—Juanita did not feel resentment. She did the boring school work willingly, and would have done much more if he had asked her to do it. She told me that she had worshipped him, and she felt that he must have been a good man because he never took advantage of her infatuation with him. He was a gentle and good man. So different, she thought, from her violent and angry father.

Secretly, at night, after her work was done, Juanita began drawing a picture of him. She did it in charcoal taken from the hearth and it came out of her like magic. She remembered that his head was balding, and that she could not show his blonde hair with the charcoal. On his body, she outlined the kinds of clothes he was likely to wear. On his shirt, she embroidered a quetzal, the Guatemalan sign of eternal good luck. And she gave him loose pants tied with rope at his thin waist.

At night when she lay down, she imagined him next to her. She felt hot in the place where she had so often seen babies come out of women. What was she feeling? She felt a strange magic as she tossed under the rough blankets. The man to whom she had given the mystical quetzal was doing this to her. It was strange but she was not afraid.

On the day before she was to return home, Juanita gave the portrait to the artist. She was very nervous because she thought he might not like it. Or maybe he would be angry with her for taking this liberty.

But, no, he took it in his hands very gently. He moved one of his hands over his face and his eyes were wet. A man was crying. Juanita was puzzled, at first. How had she hurt him, she wondered.

Finally, he said, "Juanita, this is the most beautiful gift that has ever been given to me and the technique is so fine." He told her he knew many people in the United States who did the same kind of work with charcoal. He told her to come back next summer and he would find money for her to stay in her own room instead of taking time out to run her cousin's household. She could continue to work on her painting but he would help her with the charcoal as well.

Then he told her to work hard at home over the next months until she could come back. He told her to remember what he had showed her and to do it even better. Always, he said, she should try to make the piece she was working on better than the one before, and go further with it. He said that she was very gifted and would someday be a better artist than he. When that happened he would encourage her to study under the best artists.

"No, no," Juanita said to this. "I want to work for you. I'll never get better than you. You are the teacher, I am a student."

Señor Forest must have realized how agitated his young student was. So, in the end, he urged her to work towards becoming at least as good as he was. For the time being, he felt that would be enough.

In the meantime, Juanita had to return home. She was miserable on the bus. How could she wait until next summer? It seemed like forever.

In the end, it turned out that she was back with Señor Forest sooner than either of them had expected.

When Juanita returned home, she was confronted by her father. He told her she must marry. Her mother was pregnant again and he could not afford to keep a lazy girl, he said, who did nothing but think about running away from her work to paint.

Juanita's father had a young man picked out for her and told her that she was lucky to be taken by any man, as it was getting to be known throughout the village that she was lazy. Now, this young man that Juanita's father had chosen for her was not a bad man, but he was so ordinary. She had grown up with him, seen him every day at school. All she could think of was the artist dressed in white, and his long beautiful hands. She was spoiled. She looked at the young man's hands and, she was ashamed to say, felt repulsed by their roughness. They were the hands of someone who bends over and tends the earth for his living.

As spring and the time to marry the young man grew near,

Juanita thought she would die. Then one night, she found the answer. She would run away—she would go live with the artist. Each day, she prepared herself a little bit more for leaving. She put food aside to eat on the journey. She put clothes away, little by little, in a tablecloth bundle. She found the place where her mother kept money, and stole enough to pay the bus driver.

Juanita thought it would be better not to tell her mother about her plans. The less her mother knew, the less her father could harm her. Her mother had never been able to lie to her father.

Juanita thought of all those things on the night she dipped into her mother's old cookie tin. It was slipped in behind some mud bricks where her mother piled hot tacos and beans each day as they came off the fire. Juanita was counting the money out into her hand when she heard some rustling. She swallowed hard, sure it was her father behind her. But it was her mother.

Her mother wore a long sleeping gown of light cotton. Her hair was flowing long and black as it lay on her shoulders, released from the braids she wore by day. Her belly was yet again full with child.

"Mama, you are so beautiful," Juanita said. She forgot that she was being caught stealing from her mother. All she knew was that at one time her mother had been fifteen like her, and that her mother had once had dreams like hers.

The woman reached into the cookie tin and pulled out the handkerchief of money from which Juanita had already taken some coins. Now, she placed the rest of the coins into her daughter's hand. "Goodbye, my little one," she whispered and hugged the girl for a moment, kissing the top of her head. She moved back then and her whole face shone in the moonlight with pride.

The next morning, Juanita woke herself long before dawn. She went down to the lake, took off her clothes and dipped herself in the cool water. She soaped her hair and body, until she could see herself glow. She floated on her back and saw the sun rising, taking its first steps of the day up to the top of the biggest mountain circling the lake. She knew, then, that no matter what adventures she had in her life, she would never find such a wonderful place again.

On that morning, a quetzal flew over her, and its body engraved itself in a shadow on hers. He told Juanita that good would stay with her as long as she continued to paint. He flirted with her, hinted that she should pay homage to him often in her painting. That bird was so vain. Since then, Juanita has satisfied his wish on a few occasions but not as often as he would wish. Of this one thing she is sure: the bird talked to her on that day. His words about her painting filled her with elation. She felt strong, knowing that she was doing right.

With the quetzal gone, Juanita knew she had to hurry. Her father would be up for work in the fields at any moment. She dressed carefully by the water's edge in her white cotton dress with its huge red flowers, and she brushed her hair out with her hands and braided it.

Then back to the house she went, to pick up her bundle and a package tied with string: brown paper in which she had placed her small paintings and charcoal drawings. Beside them lay a stack of freshly cooked tacos and a red ribbon from her mother's hair. She stuffed those into her pack and was gone. She never returned to her home village.

You can imagine the artist's surprise when she showed up on his doorstep. He looked down at the young woman, with her pieces of hair falling out of her braids, her pack of paintings under one arm and a bundle over her shoulder.

But all he said was, "Juanita, my dear child, you look very tired. Are you hungry? Come in and have some breakfast." Juanita could not believe his words or her own eyes. She had never heard of a man cooking for himself and a girl. And he would not hear of her helping. After they had tacos and eggs and strong coffee clouded in milk, he asked her if she would care to sleep for awhile.

First, she begged him to look at her drawings. And so he did. He sat and looked at them slowly, clearing his throat and nodding, turning them to this side and that. Sometimes, he would get up to hold the picture so that it would catch the light near the kitchen window.

"They are better," he said finally. "Now they are nearly as good as what I can do." She slept then, on the couch with a blanket he draped over her. Her sleep was one of absolute peace.

For that day things were fine, but the next morning the artist shook Juanita awake and said they were going to the village where her mother sold vegetables, to talk with her. Juanita dared not disagree. And, as it turned out, there was no reason to protest anyway. For one thing, they rode on the artist's motor bike. The wind blowing through her hair was a new sensation for Juanita. They passed people on the road and she was so proud, holding onto the back of that beautiful man. She felt she would burst open.

When they got to the market, Juanita's mother was there next to the woman who sold baskets and, on the other side, Juanita's uncle with his pots. Both Juanita and her mother were too scared to look each other in the eye but Juanita was still able to see that her mother's eyes were swollen and black and blue from her father's fist. What would happen if the artist sent her home? Her father believed that bad women deserved to be beaten—it was the only way to teach them a lesson. Juanita's escape from marriage to live with an artist must have seemed very bad to him.

The artist talked to Juanita's mother. It was still early in the day, so things were very quiet and the ears of the people in neighbouring stalls strained to hear the conversation. Señor Forest asked if it was alright for Juanita to stay near him in a pension room that he would rent. She is a very talented artist, he said, and he wanted to help her go places with her art. He said that this was his job and those were his only intentions (much to Juanita's disappointment). He would see if, at the end of the summer, he could arrange for her to study art in Guatemala City.

Juanita's mother gave the artist some of her vegetables. She was crying, but everything was alright. Juanita kissed her good-bye and they were off on the artist's bike. Its red chrome gleamed in the late morning sun and Juanita was prouder than ever.

Señor Forest told Juanita that she would stay with him for two weeks, and by then money would come from the United Nations and she could go to the pension. In the meantime, Juanita insisted on cooking his meals. He gave her his bed and he himself slept on the couch.

A week later, a letter that excited him arrived. Juanita could tell something very special would happen soon. A few days later, Señor Forest told Juanita to sit outside in the garden and try to sketch the flowers. Those particular flowers were big and red, among the green jumble of vines and leaves. They were beautiful, but Juanita knew that this task was not the artist's way of training her. He was only giving her something to do because he had no time for her on that particular day. Something else was on his mind. He would be back soon with a friend, he told her, and left.

In mid-afternoon, after Juanita had waited for hours, Señor Forest was back with a woman. Juanita was amazed when she saw this woman, who had long, gold hair, the colour of the sun coming up over the mountains in the morning. It was not blond and not red but a colour somewhere in between. Juanita has often seen this hair colour in Canada, but at that time she knew only what she had seen in her tiny village. The artist introduced the two women. The stranger's smile came from deep, deep within her clear blue eyes.

Señor Forest was so happy, he could hardly stop touching the woman. It was as if he was not quite sure she was real, as if he thought she was from one of his paintings of fantasies. Maybe he thought she would go back within the picture frame and they would be separated again—perhaps forever. Juanita wanted to paint the woman right then. It was funny, but she was not jealous of the woman. No, she merely wanted to capture some of her beauty. But, of course, she was shy—too shy to ask her to pose. Later, on the couch that night (Señor Forest had asked for his bed back), she laughed at herself for being so foolish as to think he could love a scrimp of a girl like her.

The next day, as the woman took a shower in the wooden stall set up in his backyard, Señor Forest told Juanita that the woman had agreed to help tutor her in maths and sciences and language arts. As usual, Juanita was falling behind in these subjects, for she hated them. She wanted to spend her time on painting, not on boring school things. However, it turned out that the woman was able to charm the girl into thinking school work wasn't so bad after all.

Also, the woman was good and understanding. Sometimes the artist was pushing Juanita hard now, pushing her to get better. Some days it seemed like she could not please him from the time she arrived from the pension where she was now staying, to the end of the afternoon. No matter what she did, he could not be satisfied. He would start to grow angry but then the woman would come and kiss him and Señor Forest would melt and she would say, "Juanita, time for a break. Will you join me for a walk?" And Cayenne (for that was her name) would take Juanita down to the local market, each of them swinging a yellow grass basket over her arm.

Before buying the vegetables and fruit, they would walk around and look at things and touch almost everything: the leather sandals and beaded change purses that smelled of newness; and dresses that were striped and long to the ground but stiff with embroidery at the neck and at the tops of the sleeves. At the market there was laughter and tears and noises of animals and the din of blue speckled pots and pans being sold, or stews being ladled out of them.

Then Juanita and Cayenne would look at the fruit, and they would pretend their baskets were heavier than they were so that they would have to stop for a drink, in a cafe with a roof of yellow, dried palm leaves. And sometimes Cayenne would buy Chiclets for Juanita from a wee girl who pulled at their skirts, opening her hand to display her wares. Wherever Cayenne went, it was like she owned the streets. She took them in strides, with her long legs and her tall body. She wore bright cotton dresses, silver hoop earrings and bracelets on her arms, and a similar bracelet around her left leg. Her feet were always bare.

The end of Juanita's time with the gringos came with the end of summer. It was time, the artist told Juanita, to go to Guatemala

City. He had friends in the city, with whom Juanita could stay while she attended art school there. Juanita was sad to go but excited, too. She knew it was time for her to go, and leave the artist and Cayenne alone.

But before Juanita left, she painted Cayenne out on the street with her gold-red hair flying and her legs striding down the street, in the way Juanita had so often observed. When Juanita presented her with the portrait, Cayenne threw her head back and laughed. She was delighted by the picture.

Cayenne gave Juanita a new dress she had made herself. They went for a special walk to the market where Juanita tried on sandals until they found the perfect fit, and Cayenne got her a handbag to match the footwear. From another gringo friend, Cayenne bought jeans and a plaid shirt for Juanita, so that she could fit into the modern life of a city. And, three days before Juanita left, Cayenne gave Juanita a perm. At the time, Juanita wondered about those old clothes. She, as a village girl, thought it was only proper to wear a dress in the city. Later, she felt grateful to Cayenne.

The morning she was to leave arrived, and after saying goodbye to Cayenne, Juanita hopped on the back of the artist's motorbike. She was too excited to think about never seeing Cayenne again.

It was a long way through the mountains on that bike and it was very dusty. The artist and Juanita spent the night at a hotel and on the following day they arrived in the city simply called "Guatemala" by those who live in the country.

God, the people. Juanita could feel sweat even between her legs, she was so nervous. There were people everywhere. She saw men pulling carts full of watermelons among the moving cars in the streets, and women selling food from huge caldrons on the street corners. Signs advertising jeans flashed on the street. The air was hard to breathe.

By the middle of the day, Juanita thought she would never again find one new thing that would surprise her, ever. She was wrong. The surprise came from something the artist said. After they were out on his bike again, on their way to the art school, he turned in his seat at a red traffic light. "Yes, Juanita, there's a world out there waiting for you," he said. "You go and be one with it like your ancestors. There is room for you, too, to create the monuments that defy time like the Mayans did." Juanita did not know what the hell he was talking about but, judging from the quivers in his voice, she knew it must be important.

He left her with his friends: an American man married to a rich Guatemalan of Spanish descent. When he said good bye, he kissed Juanita and told her she would someday grow into a beautiful woman. He said that when she met a man she had better make damn sure he was worthy of her.

At first, Juanita was very lonely at the art school. She was young, the youngest student at the school. The teachers and students were different, not like her artist friend. They were not so good, and cared more about talk of famous artists than being artists themselves. But she learned a lot about the old masters. She had that much to say about it.

In her second year, Juanita turned seventeen and met Rodriguez. He wore a leather jacket, had long, smooth, black hair and was very, very macho. He was involved in theatre but also took political science courses. He was surrounded by women all the time and many men, although none as good-looking as he. He was popular, and could have almost anything he wanted without trying very hard.

Juanita remembered the artist and Cayenne and that there was a whole world out there somewhere for her. Still, at night, she would toss under her blankets when she thought of Rodriguez. In the daytime, life went on.

One day, after they had first been introduced to each other, Rodriguez came over and told her of a political rally to be held by students. Would she help? Would she draw posters? Of course she would. Juanita never missed an opportunity to show her work. Rodriguez told her which slogans to use and she painted them in black letters with illustrations that she thought were powerful. Then Rodriguez told her to come to the demonstration. He told her, as if issuing an order, but at the same time he *asked* her, because he was not sure she would listen to his command.

When she did decide to attend the demonstration, he walked beside her and looked pleased with himself that she had come. Afterwards, they went to a bar to talk about what had happened. The military had come and some students were hurt, as an example for the others. Their heads were smashed with the butts of rifles. Free elections, for that is what the students were marching for, was not an idea the government and its militia (or the militia and its government—one never quite knew which organization owned the other) wanted to see catch on in the larger population.

There were many of Rodriguez' friends in the bar that evening and he was careful not to show he cared for Juanita. But, when she got up to go, he walked her home and kissed her goodnight. The kiss was so gentle that by the time Juanita recovered from her surprise, he was gone.

For two weeks, Juanita saw nothing of Rodriguez except one glimpse of him from a long way across the square when she was hurrying to the studio classroom. Then, one night, he showed up at her place. He asked her to go to a film with him, and she said yes. The American and his wife did not like the looks of him, but they said Juanita could go if she returned early.

The film was an old one: Marlon Brando in *On the Waterfront*. Juanita couldn't keep her mind on the storyline. She was too worried about the man who was sitting next to her to appreciate the movie star on the screen. She wanted Rodriguez to put his arm around her but she felt she would die of shyness if he did. He sat instead with his arm loose on the back of her seat and his legs spread wide apart. His eyes, she thought, were probably fixed on the screen in disapproval of what he was seeing, but she did not dare look at him to see if she could read his thoughts on his face. She wished she had accepted the drink he had offered to buy her before the show started. She was sweating and her throat was dry. Then, he was moving his arm closer and she did not know what to do about it. One of her legs was falling asleep but she was afraid to move it.

Juanita never found out where his arm would have finally rested or what the film was about—and certainly not how it ended. Years later, in Winnipeg, she heard it was going to be shown at the art gallery. Rodriguez and she went, but the film had not arrived in time so it was replaced by another.

This first time, the film was interrupted halfway through by the military. Three men in uniform came into the theatre and shot two men sitting directly in front of Juanita and Rodriguez.

Juanita sat paralysed in her seat, as she witnessed for the first time a terrible fact of life about her homeland. Since that time she has been witness to many deaths and she has always felt the same way.

She felt nothing. There were no feelings big enough for her so she simply felt nothing.

Then Rodriguez grabbed her hand and they ran. They ran and ran until she thought they could not run anymore, ever. This was the first day of their years of running together. Juanita called it the beginning of their marriage as two people who would run for revolution.

On that first day, the running ended in Rodriguez' room. The door had barely been closed behind them before Juanita began to paw at his jacket and pull it off. They said nothing. Juanita needed to feel something again. She needed to feel that she could still feel. Nothing mattered. They were alive and they held each other. They were alive. It didn't hurt. It was the first time for Juanita but it did not hurt. They made love over and over again until dawn.

In the morning, Juanita went to the phone centre, waited in line and finally called the American and his wife to tell them she was alive. At breakfast, in a cafe down the street from the phone centre, Juanita told Rodriguez she would do anything to stop the military from killing people. When he asked if she would even kill, she replied, yes, she would even kill.

She got up and left him. She knew he would contact her when it was necessary for him to do so.

A few months later, Juanita found herself in the jungle with a gun strap across her breasts and belly, and a child growing inside. That gun took the place of the paintbrush in her hand, for a long, long time.

TARA

In Paphos, in Cyprus, a road winds up from the waterfront. It leads me back to my flat when I return from picking up the paper and doing my banking in the morning or from walks at night.

The road is lined with shops. Each sells landscape postcards and tacky souvenirs. Cards of middle-aged women dressed in respectable black, and pulling loaves of heavy brown bread from outdoor ovens surrounded by fields of yellow flowers, mingle with tee-shirts of Mickey Mouse in a beach chair. This merchandise hangs on racks that clutter the elevated cement sidewalks and make my passage up the hill slow and erratic.

As I step around dozens of dangling miniature dolls in traditional Greek costumes, I almost collide with an elderly woman who has been scaring me since the beginning of my stay here.

She is one of the ancients from Britain, here to escape the winter draft in her mother country. Her skin hangs down both sides of her face where it must have once stretched over plump cheeks. It is heavily rouged. I feel embarrassed for her attempt at paint-on beauty. I want to look away but my eyes are attached to her like they would be to a horror movie.

She propels herself by me and, as I back away from her, I see she is wearing a grey fur coat—Persian lamb—which hangs draped over her gaunt body and humped back. The stick she holds in one hand serves as a break to stop her from sliding down the hill to her death. But I can see there is no turning back for this woman. I suppress the urge to push her down the hill.

Suddenly she is startled, and behind her thick steel-rimmed

glasses I see clear blue points of recognition break through her clouded eyes. Her smile is a grimace. It looks like she is in pain from straining the muscles in the corners of her lips.

She pants and so do I. For if she recognizes me as being someone she knew in her past, I am terrified that she will be my future. I try to run but I bump into a rack.

Look at her, a voice suddenly tells me. It is Lou's voice. *Turn and watch her. What are you afraid of?*

I force myself to turn as she slowly recedes down the hill.

You know my story. Lou makes a clucking sound with her tongue. *It's for you to know and then it is your responsibility to pass it on. You owe me, you owe us, for our stories from the past will make your journey into the future easier. I was never one to mince words. YOU OWE US.*

Lou's insistent voice reminds me of her existence, and of how I came to know her. It was after I began to jot Juanita's story in my green notebook, and I was eager to see Juanita again to hear more. I was like an addict. But, as had happened on the previous occasions we had talked, I wanted to combine work for the cause with storytelling.

I must admit, this was a familiar story during all the time I had my life deeply wound up in the feminist movement. I would want to make friends with someone but there would be wide gaps between the times we could both get together to talk and laugh and share bits of our lives—even the painful parts.

So Juanita and I met Lou for the first time when we were sitting behind a table of Women for Equality brochures and tee-shirts during the International Women's Day celebrations. It was in a downtown shopping mall on a Saturday and we were there with a bunch of other tables displaying literature for a number of women's groups. It should have been busy but it wasn't because the weather outside was building into a blizzard.

Juanita and I had talked about packing up and leaving when a swirl of wind pushed an elderly woman through the outside doors close to where we were set up. She stood panting by the entrance for a few moments until she was able to catch her breath and regain her composure. I remember staring at her as her nose visibly pulled air into her lungs.

Then she began unzipping the navy blue ski-doo suit in which her small frame was clad. When she pulled down her hood, I saw a head of snow white, softly curled hair surrounding her pale pink face, which was gently wrinkled.

In her pocket, she dug around for a moment and then pulled out a pair of glasses which she deftly placed on her nose. The frames were pale blue with a few sparkles running through them but, settled on her nose, they did not appear at all gaudy.

She then stepped out of her ski-doo suit altogether. She wore a pale blue tee-shirt with the familiar pro-choice logo on it. Her legs were clad in pale pink jogging pants. When I got to know Lou better, I realized that she almost always wore those colours: pale blues and pinks and whites.

With her ski-doo suit tucked under her arm, she approached our table. She glanced at the organization's name sign and then scrutinized the two of us carefully for a moment before speaking.

"How do I become associated with your cause?" she demanded.

"Well ... you would take out a membership, I guess," I said, a bit confused. I wasn't sure what she meant. Most people simply asked how to become a member.

"Yes, of course, I would take out a membership," she said, as if I was either being nonsensical or a complete idiot. "But what I really want to do is tell my story. I want to leave my story behind when I go."

Juanita laughed. "Tara is the one to talk to," she said.

"Oh, very well ... here is what I will do," the old woman continued, after she had sized me up for a moment. "I shall fill out your membership form." Having done that, she rummaged in the pocket of her ski-doo suit and rescued a little brown change purse with a gold clasp. She pulled out a five- and a ten-dollar bill and handed them to me along with the form.

I looked it over. "Call me 'Lou'," she said. "I detest being called ' Mrs.'... Now, when can I make an appointment with you to begin?"

"Monday, I guess." I knew there would be no way to stall her.

"At what time?"

"Ten o'clock?"

"Fine ... and you said your name was?"

"Tara."

"Very well ... Monday at ten. I can't stay and chat now. I must get back home before the storm gets worse." She donned her ski-doo suit and left, and we left shortly after.

Ten o'clock Monday morning descended upon me. I am not a morning person in the first place, and with the International Women's Day celebrations continuing for that whole week I was very busy. I think I was in charge of making up slogans for signs that Juanita would paint for our march and rally at the legislature the following Saturday. The phone was ringing off the hook as usual and some courier was standing in front of me wanting to get paid for a delivery. As I rummaged through our little, green, metal cashbox with one hand and held the phone in the other, I wished Lou would be the type of old person who forgets things.

But I knew she wasn't. And sure enough, there she was, standing next to my desk on the dot of ten o'clock. And after an hour had gone by she left just as promptly, after setting up an appointment with me for the following Monday.

This went on for about a month-and-a-half until I suggested she should start coming at eleven so we could go for lunch together after the hour was up. You see, as she told me more about herself I grew to like Lou more and more.

Now, back in Cyprus, I turn quickly towards my flat. "Think about Lou and you won't be afraid," I repeat to myself, like a child who wants something very badly. I enter my flat and then rush over to where my typewriter is set up on the round dining-room table.

I begin to write about Lou. I get two-and-a-half pages into her story before I allow myself to stop and take a satisfying sigh. I am no longer afraid. Lou is good for me.

LOU

When Lou was very young—just turning three—her parents decided to move the family from Iceland to Canada. Both Lou's father and mother had relatives already living in Winnipeg and the interlake parts of Manitoba.

Lou recalled nothing of their voyage to Canada by ship, and nothing of the train ride to Winnipeg. Her earliest memory was of the blizzard in which they found themselves upon their arrival.

Outside it was cold enough to take one's breath away. "Bitterly cold," Lou remembered, but nonetheless she found it extremely invigorating as the hard, icy snow pricked the bare skin of her face—the only part of her body not covered by woolens.

In the middle of this blizzard, the little girl wandered outside alone and was picked up by the wind and deposited somewhere down the street from the place on Main Street where her aunt and uncle lived. Soon her woolens did not protect her from the cold. Her fingers and toes grew numb.

Through squinting eyes, Lou looked for shelter. She made out the brown frame of a huge barn and noticed a door. The blizzard blew her closer, but it took all her strength to pull out the bar that held the door closed.

Inside the barn it was hot, and the air was moist. A cloud of steam drifted around her face. As her eyes grew accustomed to the dark, she noticed a horse, breathing out steam just as she was. She imagined that the steam was smoke and that the horse was somehow supernatural, a fire-burning, smoke-breathing animal.

Soon the little girl's skin felt sticky with humidity. She

unravelled her outer garments of brown and beige sheep's wool, and pulled off her blue mitts and hat. She curled up next to the dappled horse and fell asleep.

She woke to her father shaking her, so hard that she felt sure she would be left without her skin. They had been searching for her all night, he said. He and Lou's mother were beside themselves with anguish. When he was through scolding her, he folded his youngest child in his arms and carried her back to where her mother and brother were waiting with her aunt and uncle.

Lou paid a price for her wanderings. By the next morning she had "come down with something," as they say. It turned out to be pneumonia, and it attacked her with a fierceness that kept her ill in bed for months and left her recuperating for several more.

In the meantime, Lou's parents had obtained land which they intended to clear for farming out near Winnipeg Beach. Nothing could be done there until spring, however. Savings were dwindling so Lou's mother took on the position of a maid at a wealthy home in the Wolesley part of the city and her father got a job as a manservant at another private residence nearby. He took Lou's brother with him as a sort of assistant. And, when Lou had recovered sufficiently, she left the house of her aunt and uncle to be with her mother.

This wasn't an easy time for Lou's mother, who had to keep a three-storey dwelling clean, assist the cook and serve at the table, all with a small child at her heels. Yet, she did this for several winters. Establishing a farm on the marginal land on the west side of Lake Winnipeg wasn't easy either.

Of that time, Lou remembered two things which foretold two important associations she would make.

The first thing was a recurring dream. In the dream, she would see a face. The face would change. Sometimes it belonged to a girl. At other times, it was a boy, a man, or a woman. Sometimes the face was familiar. At other times, it was the face of a stranger.

But the eyes were always a piercing sea-blue.

Once in a while, Lou would wake from the dream with an

uneasy feeling. Most times, the dream made her feel peaceful and contented.

The other portent of the future was an event. Nellie Mc-Clung, the famous suffragist, was a friend of the woman for whom Lou's mother worked. It was because of this connection that Lou and her mother found themselves down at the Morris Stampede one hot summer weekend. Their mistress had volunteered their services to Nellie and the others who had set up an information booth at the stampede.

Lou was sent to handbill the crowds of people and do anything she could to lure them over to the booth, where the suffragists would then coax and persuade them into signing their names on a petition. The petition was to be presented to the government as part of the lobby for the women's franchise.

Lou's face was itchy with sweat and dust by the time she got around to passing out leaflets to a group of cowboys waiting their turns in the chuckwagon races. She was shy, but felt it was improper to leave anyone out because the cause was so important, she knew, to her mother and the other women at the booth.

She handed out the literature and turned to walk quickly away.

"Hey, you!" one cowboy called. Lou considered running.

"Hey, you." She felt a hand on her shoulder. She turned, then, and looked up at the sunburned face of a very tall cowboy.

"Who told you to give these away?"

"Mrs. McClung."

"Well, you tell this McClung lady that she ain't no lady because no lady would be hankering after the vote."

"Why not?" another cowboy—this one in a bright green and red shirt—interrupted. "My mother goes out to vote in California and I reckon she's a lady ... Little girl, show me the way to the booth."

The cowboy had a broad smile and he even gave Lou a drink out of his canteen.

The rest of the day passed uneventfully. Finally, Lou's mother told her she could play until they were packed up and ready to return to the rooming house for the night.

Relieved of her work, Lou found renewed energy and raced off to climb the bleachers, to which people were returning after their supper break. One end of the bleachers was absolutely clear so Lou chose to ascend to the top of that area. Up, up, up fifteen steps she went.

When she got to the top, Lou saw the sun setting in the west. Purple, orange, yellow, red, light grey and blue filled the horizon.

"You will again do work of significance to women before your life is completed," a cultivated voice predicted.

Lou shook her head and laughed. She wondered how the voice had found its way into her ears.

Eventually, Lou's family was able to move out to the farm permanently. Lou grew into her teens doing the things most young people did on the farm in those days. She helped with the never-ending chores, went to school in a one-room building a two-mile walk away and read or studied by lamplight in the evenings.

On the Christmas of her eighteenth year, Lou and her family celebrated the day with the aunt and uncle who lived right down by the lake. Lou remembered feeling bored that holiday season. After all, if they had spent Christmas in the city she might have had the opportunity to see a certain young man once again. He had been particularly attentive to her at a similar gathering in the fall.

After the noonday meal and despite the blizzard that had begun to blow, Lou left the monotony of washing the dishes to the older women and slipped quietly out into the storm.

It did not take her long to find her way out onto the ice of the lake. At least, she supposed she was out on the lake. It was difficult to determine where the bank left off and where the lake began when everything was covered in snow. It was not long before Lou found herself wandering through the blank white, the nothingness. And soon she began to grow edgy, to worry that the weather was about to betray her and she would lose herself in it.

Then she saw a grey shape coming towards her. She stood still, hoping it would find her. The shape turned into a man. "Oh, there you are," Lou said, as if she knew him intimately, although she had never met him before.

His piercing blue eyes were those of her dreams.

By springtime Lou was married to the man, who had been coming back from ice-fishing on that Christmas day. His name was Jake and he had just arrived in Winnipeg Beach to manage a local store that was left to him by his grandfather. On that Christmas afternoon he had escorted Lou up to the store where they both warmed their frostbitten hands over the black pot-bellied stove. They had warmed their insides with a bit of scotch, and it was then they began to talk. Both had admitted to being foolish for going out onto the lake in a winter storm. The conversation lead elsewhere, and their relationship progressed nicely from there.

After the wedding, Lou joined Jake in the two rooms he had already set up in the back of the store. There was no going away for a honeymoon. People in small towns depended on their general store for so many things, and counted on it being open; besides, there was no money for such a frivolity.

Lou and Jake established a routine very quickly. Each morning, he would open up the front while she cleaned the breakfast things and tidied their living quarters.

Then, she would go up front, where Jake would fill her hands with dusting cloths to clean off the tinned goods, or scrub-pails to use while scouring the wood floors on her hands and knees. And when her husband had to be out, maybe on a trip into the city for supplies or perhaps to help a neighbour with his commercial fishing, it was Lou who stood behind the till to serve the customers.

Lou loved this work. A customer would ask her to scoop two pounds of sugar out of the bag leaning against the counter, or would request a slice of orange cheese off the half moon that sat on display under its glass cover on the front counter. Lou filled these orders and chatted with the customer.

She was shy in the beginning, but soon overcame this. In their discussions, she and the customers would solve the Depression, contemplate the problems brewing in Europe, predict the fishing season's outcome, and speculate on how the young Ukrainian widow who lived down the road and dyed her hair red managed to make a living. It was a pleasure to exchange ideas with other human beings and Lou looked forward to each working day.

Later in bed at night, Jake and Lou would talk about the matters brought to their attention during the day, among other things. And Lou soon became pregnant.

During the first few months of the pregnancy Lou felt content, complete within herself, full of a peaceful power. Then into her life came a disruption, harder to endure but just as shocking as a slap in the face.

Jake's two old maiden aunts arrived, to be with her in her confinement. They fussed about how improper it was for Lou to be standing out in front and serving the public when "it" was so obvious. What kind of husband was Jake for allowing other men to see her in her condition? On and on they went until Jake took their side and ordered Lou to stay in the back rooms.

Once they had Lou closeted in the living quarters, Jake's aunts would not let up until they had imprisoned her in bed. Lou gave up. Even her anger towards Jake for not intervening on her behalf died. She felt the extreme tiredness of the late stages of pregnancy. It was difficult to even think about doing anything, let alone insist on getting out of bed when everyone around her was determined to keep her in it.

The result, of course, was that by the time she went into labour Lou's body was weak and ill-fit for the work expected of it. She was deeply depressed, too. Only the thought of the baby inside gave her the will to ride the pain and push him out.

Still, she was not performing in the way Jake's aunts felt she should be. They wanted her to push when she felt no urge. The baby should be out by now. The baby was in trouble. The labour was too long. They went on and on. Lou tensed up.

The doctor was called in to intervene. He ripped the baby out of her, and she bled for hours. Only the desire to care for that little, helpless baby gave Lou the will to live.

However, the aunts had not finished torturing Lou. She was to remain closeted in the backrooms until her son, whom she named Peter, had been weaned. If allowing the public to see her pregnant was risque, then baring her breasts to a hungry infant was a hundred times more so. Besides, what kind of a provider would Jake look like if his wife was out there working so soon after confinement? Scrubbing out dirty diapers in the back was more appropriate.

Finally, around the time that Peter began to crawl, the old women liberated Lou. They packed their bags and took the train back to the city. By that time, she felt like a caged bird, too frightened to go outside her cage even when the door is left wide open. When working out in the front again, Lou could hardly bring herself to utter "yes" and "no" to anyone who asked her a direct question. Nodding her head was about as much as she could handle. She was scared of those people who walked in from the huge terrifying world and talked of the weather in booming voices. She no longer understood how she had functioned and even enjoyed being out there with the public before her confinement.

But the child wanted to venture further out into the world. When people would leave, banging the screen door behind them, he would wobble over to the door. He would stop there a moment and then go back to tug on his mother's hand. When summer came, Lou could resist his pull no longer.

There were pink roses on the path leading down to the lake, and mother and son would walk towards them in the splendour of the afternoon sun. Once out there, Lou spotted the blueberries growing along the path. Mother and child would sit down among those bushes as she popped the berries into her son's mouth.

Gradually, Lou began to notice the world flowing out around her again. She began to take Peter out to gather blueberries in the tin pails that had once held screws and nails in the hardware section of the store. At first they picked close to home, but gradually they ventured further west.

It was in those bushes that Lou and her little boy stumbled upon the Ukrainian woman with the dyed-red hair. They had been moving along, Lou picking and singing to Peter, who was always slightly ahead of her as they migrated from one blueberry patch to another.

Suddenly, Peter began to toddle off more quickly than usual, and Lou looked up. And there he was, within arm's length of the Ukrainian widow, with one finger pointed at her red hair while he smiled back at his mother in delight. The woman seemed as delighted as the child. She cooed and gently pinched his cheeks. Lou came up and the two women, both a bit shy, reached out to shake hands after wiping them clean of burgundy stains. The woman introduced herself as Eva.

As if feeling pressure to waste no time, Eva immediately stooped down again and continued to pick. Lou saw several pails, but only one or two were filled with berries. The others were filled with different plants, twigs, lichens and even mushrooms.

It was obvious that Eva was too busy to talk about the things she had harvested from the bush, so Lou did not ask questions. Instead, she brought her pail over and picked berries near the other woman. They said nothing but they did keep each other company.

Often, after that first meeting, Peter and Lou would come upon Eva in one part of the bush or another. She would straighten up from her work when they arrived and push the pink, flowered kerchief away from her forehead onto her shoulders. Then she would rest her hands on her wide hips and talk with Lou for maybe five minutes. It was only small talk but it drew the women closer and closer together as the days went on. Sometimes Eva would reach into her skirt pocket and pull out a piece of poppyseed cake, carefully wrapped in a snow white hanky with fine blue and yellow flowers embroidered on its edges. This was for Peter, who held out his hand expectantly. (At home he called her "the cake and berry lady").

Then she would resume her picking. Lou remembered that Eva's hands moved so fast, Lou was sometimes unable to tear her eyes away from them for several minutes.

In the store, the gossip about Eva would continue from time to time. Often the things said were very cruel. One day, a man who had come back from a morning in the city stopped by the store. He mentioned seeing that "scarlet-haired Hunky woman" out by the roadside selling her berries and "no doubt a few other things as well." He laughed, but Lou deliberately reached over and covered Peter's ears with her hands. At that, the man walked out in a bit of a huff. Lou didn't care. Business was not that bad.

When the berry season was over, Lou found herself spending more time in the store again. Her confidence in herself had returned, and she once more enjoyed listening and talking to those who brought news of the world, whether it was something occurring in faraway India or an event in Gimli, the town to the north.

On slow afternoons, Lou would sometimes read. Other days, if she could persuade Jake to look out for Peter, she would go out to teas and bake sales hosted by one church group or another. She would go to see what the latest fashions were—a school teacher from the city who had been hired to work in Winnipeg Beach always seemed to sport the new styles and never failed to attend the community functions. The talk, though, was generally boring.

Still, with these things occupying Lou's time, thoughts of Eva were pushed to the back of her mind until a certain day in mid-autumn. On that day, a note came in the mail, addressed to Lou in spindly handwriting. It turned out to be an invitation from Eva to come for tea and to bring her "beautiful son." On the back of the cream-coloured note paper with its thin light-blue border, she had drawn a map of the sand roads that led to her house. It was located up west above the main road to the city, but was still not very far from the store.

Lou took out some of the nicest letter paper they sold in the store. It was bright yellow, and each page had pansies in the corner. She quickly dashed off a letter to Eva, accepting the invitation for tea, and saw that it was posted on the same afternoon.

When the day for tea with Eva arrived, Lou told Jake that Peter had been listless and that she felt it would be good for him to walk in the fresh October air. She did not want to tell her husband the truth because she feared he would refuse to let her go. After all, gossip about Eva had been vicious.

So Lou and little Peter went to Eva's house on a bright, crisp October day splattered with the gold, orange and red of turning leaves. Eva's "house" was actually a cabin, made out of logs that had been varnished the deep-brown colour of burned toast.

To one side of the house was a small field. The earth here had been turned over with a shovel, and only some corn stalks, marrow vines and a few cabbages remained from what must have been a gigantic garden. At the back edge of the garden, mother and son could see Eva hacking away at bushes with an axe.

"Eva," Lou yelled and waved a greeting, while Peter scrambled across the garden towards her. "So you have come," she said and shook Peter's little hand before slinging the axe over one shoulder and dragging the bushes behind her to where Lou stood. To Peter she gave a scrawny twig because he, of course, wanted to help. Then, with Lou and Peter walking beside her, Eva pulled the bushes around to the other side of the cabin and put them on top of the charred remnants of those bushes she had already burned. "There," she said. "Too many bushes. I do not like to have them crowd me in ... Come." She motioned Lou and the boy to follow her into the house.

When they first stepped inside, Lou found the smells quite overpowering. On the walls of what turned out to be the kitchen, living and dining rooms all rolled into one, were hanging garlands of dill, garlic and herbs. On the counter, next to the chipped, white-enamel wash basin in which Eva rinsed her green-stained hands, were rows of jars filled with dill pickles. The vinegar that had gone into their canning still clung to the air.

Eva wiped her hands on the apron around her waist and quickly picked up four of the jars, holding them to her bosom. These she carried over to a door with a large piece of yellow rope strung through a hole in its wood. She used the rope as a handle and opened the door. Lou, looking over Eva's shoulder, could make out rows and rows of canned beets, cabbage, raspberries, blueberries—all sorts of things.

Eva pushed some jars over to make room for her pickles and pulled out a jar of chokecherry jelly before she closed the door. The jelly she set down beside the solitary sealer of pickles she had left out on the counter. These she gave to Lou when Lou was about to leave later that afternoon.

"Come, sit," she said. Then Lou noticed the table, laden with pots and bowls that were covered with flour-sack tea towels— some of the towels were off-white, some had tiny blue floral patterns, others had orange daisies. All these items were jammed together on the shiny blue-checked tablecloth.

Eva started to uncover things and steam rose up from platters of perogies (filled, Lou later discovered, with a variety of things: cottage cheese, potatoes, blueberries and even raisins), cabbage rolls, and buns filled with juicy prunes. There was boiled chicken and hot tea and figs stewing in their own juices and bowls of pickles and salads. The bread was a bright yellow and rich with eggs. It was a feast, spread out for Lou and her round-eyed little boy.

"Sit," Eva urged, and then, "Eat." Eat they did, and Eva enjoyed watching them eat—even more, Lou thought, than the two guests enjoyed demolishing that feast. Eva sat with her hands holding her aproned belly and once or twice she leaned over, grabbed Peter's red little cheeks and kissed one and then the other.

When they had finished gorging on the food in front of them, Eva brought out sponge cake doused in strawberries. This they savoured, along with cups of tea.

Eva sipped on the tea, cleared her throat and began to talk. She had come from the Ukraine with her husband, she told Lou, only days after they had been married. They came in a cargo ship and slept, when they could, among the wooden crates and barrels in the hull.

Her husband, Horace, had paid a great deal of money to the ship's captain for them to be transported to this country, where homesteader's land was waiting for him. In the Ukraine, there was really no land for Horace. His family's land had been divided so often from father to son down the line that there was nothing for Horace larger than a plot big enough to build a house on, and perhaps enough room for a garden. So they came to Canada.

They wound up in Winnipeg Beach. The land marked on the map in Horace's name was large compared to what he had left behind in the old country, but it was filled with evergreen trees, bushes and huge rocks. It presented a different picture than the one he had carried in his mind from stories he had heard. In his imagination, he had seen his land to be a huge wheat field stretching out over the prairies as far as the eye could see.

But the land was theirs, Horace and Eva told each other on the morning after they had spent their first night sleeping under the trees on their land. They worked for weeks building the cabin. And it took months and months to clear the garden and cut down trees further into the bush, where Horace wanted his wheat to grow.

Then, unexpectedly, disaster struck. Horace accidentally felled a tree on top of himself. It crushed the life out of him too quickly for him to even bid Eva goodbye. All by herself, she managed to drag the tree off him and was halfway through digging out a grave for the body when a neighbour happened by.

The neighbour, an old bachelor, was quite kind to her at first. He finished digging the grave, all the while telling her about the lonely life he led.

Horace and Eva had been studying English together night after night, so she had little trouble understanding the old man's words. But she did not understand the deeper implications of what he was saying. Finally, he asked her how she expected to live with her husband gone. She hadn't had time to think, she said. The man looked into her worried eyes and told her not to fret. He would see to it that she would have what she needed.

He waited a month, though, until he came around again. By that time, Eva's supplies—the dried meat, millet, pearl barley and other necessities they had brought over from the old country—were very nearly gone. Horace's savings were dwindling, too, what with Eva supplementing the seeds they had brought from the Ukraine with store-bought ones. There were a few other absolute necessities she had bought, and it was still a few months before the garden would bear vegetables. The berries in the bushes were only beginning to ripen. This was Eva's state when the man returned. He brought with him some canned goods and a chunk of fresh deer meat for her.

"But I have no money to pay," Eva protested, although her mouth watered as she looked at the plump red strawberries on the label of one of the tins.

"You have something better than money for a bachelor like me," he said and fought her down to the dirt floor.

And that is how Eva survived until her garden came in, and then she barred her door when the man came around with food again. He did not press her further.

However, Eva did become pregnant. She did not have to go to the doctor to find this out. Her breasts began to hurt and her periods stopped. She knew she was pregnant.

She thought back to a woman she knew who had lived on the edge of the Ukrainian town where Eva grew up. The woman had lived in a small cottage there. Each fall she would go out into the surrounding fields and woods where she would gather the plants, seeds, mushrooms and twigs that would provide the medicines people often sought from her.

Eva recalled one particular night when she was quite small. Her father was not home, and her mother bundled her up in a shawl and took her along to this woman's house. Once there, Eva's mother had a quiet conversation with the woman. In a minute, the woman had produced a dried plant that Eva's mother wrapped in a handkerchief and stuffed into a skirt pocket.

As Eva was growing up, she sometimes got bored and ended up looking in the drawer where her mother kept her underwear. She would find the plant there. Its smell had stayed with her, a memory in her nostrils.

So Eva went out into the bushes of the Manitoba interlake to search for that plant. Her hands were moist with the sweat of relief when she found it. Back home, she brewed it like tea.

After cups and cups of the brewed plant, Eva's menses flowed once more. Surely, she thought, God in his mercy would understand. The women in her hometown had whispered the same words to each other after each visit to the woman on the edge of the town.

As she told Lou about it, on that afternoon of their first "tea" together, Eva's voice still took on a thankful tone and her hands and shoulders relaxed in relief. She recalled her elation at being free of the bachelor's domination.

Lou left Eva that day with a resolve to visit as often as she could get away from the store. But that year it was early November when the harsh winter began and Lou was soon busy preparing for Christmas. With the usual baking and decorating, her time was filled.

By the end of January, though, the festivities came to an abrupt halt for Lou in a very personal way. She rose early one morning, rushed over to the corner where the toilet pail stood and vomited into it. Jake and Peter were still asleep.

It was storming outside so Lou put on her husband's great-coat and her own boots, and bundled up in woolens. Out she went with the pail. She dumped the contents in the outhouse hole and continued on her way.

As she headed west, the snow blew like pellets against her face. Somehow, they made her angry. Her anger began to focus in on specific people. First, she felt angry towards Jake, who had not protected her from his meddling aunts. They were as over-bearing as always. She had seen them in the city over Christmas, and had tried to avoid them as much as possible at family gatherings. She knew that she would never be able to stand up to them. And then she was angry at her doctor. Even the doctor had bowed to their wishes. During those first few months after little Peter was born, she had thought often about killing herself. With a small boy and another baby, things might prove too much for her. She might go insane. Better not to have children if you couldn't take care of them.

And how would little Peter remember her? Would he grow up to hate the memory of his weakling mother? And what if he should happen to be left to the guidance of Jake's old aunts?

No, Lou told the winter storm when she stopped to rest in the shelter of a pine tree for a moment. No, she would not go into confinement again. Being out in the store serving customers was her connection to the world. The work was hard but it allowed her to participate in talk of politics and religion and life and death and marriage and birth—yes, birth.

Suddenly, she tried to run. She didn't get far, for her feet stuck in the deep snow. She began to whimper like a small child. Then she howled, tears streaming down her cheeks. Through those tears she looked up and saw something dark hovering in front of her.

It was Eva's cabin. In her despair, Lou had wandered all the way to her friend's door. The blizzard had shown her the way to the one person who could help her.

Lou pounded on the door and Eva answered it. She felt the warmth of the room and the warmth in Eva's eyes, even as Eva recognized Lou in Jake's oversized clothes. Eva pulled her inside and took off Lou's outdoor things before the fireplace, as she might have done with a child. She pulled her shawl closer and involuntarily shivered at the mere look of all the snow caked on Lou's outer garments. Soon there was a cup of tea in Lou's hand.

"Now, you have come to me for help," Eva said. Somehow, she knew.

Lou visited Eva regularly after that. In time, Lou and her husband were able to make their little store business prosper, and eventually they decided to move into the city where they felt educational opportunities were better for young Peter. They sold the store at Winnipeg Beach and bought another in the Wolesley area of Winnipeg, familiar to Lou from her childhood.

One day, as Lou stood behind the counter in their new corner store, a woman walked in and asked if she could leave some birth control pamphlets on the counter, where women who came to shop for groceries would see them. She introduced herself as Mary Speechly.

Around the time when Lou and Mary Speechly met, poverty from the Depression had reached epidemic proportions on the

Prairies. It touched the wealthy Wolesley residents in the form of transients—mostly young, unemployed men who were searching for jobs—who often ended up at their backdoors, begging for a meal. Many drifted into Lou's store as well.

Women like Mary Speechly understood that many of these young unemployed men had left pregnant wives and small children back home. And it was these young women who had to watch their children go without when the vegetables they had put away from the previous summer had run out, and they had long since slaughtered the cattle and chickens—even the ones that would, in good years, be used to keep the stock reproducing.

Mary, and women like her, looked around and refused to close their eyes to the suffering. In fact, in order to see more clearly, they had the public health nurses take them through the working class parts of the city and out to the surrounding rural areas. And when they saw the desperation, they wanted to right the wrongs as quickly as possible.

Mary Speechly and Mrs. Charles Steacy and a handful of others in Winnipeg became firm in their convictions that smaller families were the answer. Rich women had always known this, it seemed. Now it was time to help less wealthy women, so that they could help themselves and their families out of poverty. Mary and the other women felt it was up to them to reach out to their sisters. After all, Prime Minister Bennett's government could not be depended upon.

So when Lou met Mary Speechly, she too became involved. She said that it would be more discreet to keep the pamphlets under the counter. She could quietly slip them in among the groceries when she packed the women customers' bags.

Lou read the pamphlet after Mary left. She sat for quite some time mulling over the address at the bottom of the pamphlet. Finally, she made a decision. Peter was old enough to be left in charge of the store by this time, so Lou was able to go out for a few hours.

The address turned out to be the room of the community health nurse and it was from her that Lou purchased a supply of contraceptive jelly and condoms.

Shortly after Lou had made this trip, Mary Speechly happened into the store again. Lou invited her into the back for some coffee and blueberry muffins. She volunteered to involve herself in Mary's cause. Mary welcomed Lou into the crusade and explained a few things about her group, the Winnipeg Birth Control Society, and what it was doing.

Once they had decided upon the need for such a society, Mary said, it had fallen upon her shoulders as president of the Winnipeg Birth Control Society to correspond with a Mr. A.R. Kaufman of Kitchener, Ontario. This particular gentleman, they had heard on good authority, produced condoms and other birth control supplies at his rubber factory.

In due course, Kaufman responded to Mary's letter and agreed to supply qualified community health nurses in the Winnipeg area with whatever they needed to meet the demand for birth control out in the West. Since then, Mary explained to Lou, Mr. Kaufman had kept his word, and with little remuneration. The Winnipeg Birth Control Society had next to no money and usually found itself quite incapable of paying him.

Mr. Kaufman was very dedicated to their cause in Winnipeg, Mary said (and her eyes glowed at the very thought of him), and indeed, almost anywhere else in Canada where the dissemination of birth control information was creating the need for supplies.

At the conclusion of their discussion, Mary thanked Lou for volunteering and told her the BCS was always more than happy to be offered another pair of helping hands. She asked if Lou would take minutes at the meetings until the group's regular secretary returned from a holiday overseas. Lou said she would be delighted to do so.

The BCS meetings were held at the Legislative Buildings, with the consent of the provincial government. Lou had educated herself in politics during all those conversations that went on with customers in the store, so when she became active in the BCS, it did not take her long to arrive at an opinion as to why the provincial government was so generous in providing the group with meeting space.

She came to suspect that the provincial government, like the federal government, was hoping the BCS and other similar groups across the country would solve the problems of poverty. The dominion government, which had helped to create the poverty, had not a clue as to how it could be eliminated.

For decades, Canadian politicians and bureaucrats had been advocating the population of the west. When they could no longer entice "the right kind of immigrants" of "fine British stock" then "the right kind of immigrants" became the Eastern Europeans—those young Ukrainian men and women who could populate the west with farm labourers, factory workers and servant girls.

It was made perfectly clear, however, that this third wave of immigrants (after those of British stock and the Icelanders) were to help the first wave—who were those in power—to prosper. So the new immigrants were reminded often of their proper place in society. Clearly the uppercrust believed that these immigrants did not have the mental capacity to run things.

Or did they? The 1919 Winnipeg General strike had come as a surprise to some, and the people in power had put their own interpretation on the event: some "wayward Brits of the lowest classes" had been guided into rebellion under the influence of the "Bolsheviks." Now, with the Depression, unrest was brewing among the unemployed. The very principles of the free world could be at stake once again. What the British empire had fought for, what her sons had died for, was on the verge of crumbling.

The attitude of the "haves" made Lou's blood curdle. She came to believe that the government was hoping the BCS would do what it could not. After all, how could the government continue a campaign to decrease the population after propagating so many deceitful lies to bring those same immigrants over to Canada in the first place? No one's memory was that short. Surely the immigrants could remember the promises of endless acres of land in an always-warm climate. They would not tolerate an enforced limit to their offspring now, in order to appease those who had done them so many bad turns.

But perhaps, members of the legislature must have thought, Mary Speechly and the others could do their dirty work for them. And, being women, they would almost certainly do it for nothing. What could the government possibly lose? Allowing them a meeting place at the Legislature was a small price to pay.

Lou theorized about all this, but she was absolutely sure about at least one thing: Mary and her colleagues had begun their work in response to the voices of women. They had been unable to ignore the pleas of women. The pleas came from women on the farms, who were so isolated that they often had to bear children without the aid of a midwife or doctor. And they came from women in factories who knew of their sisters bleeding to death in childbirth and feared that they, too, would meet this fate the next time. There were some women who were never taught about healthy sexuality but still knew something was wrong in their relations with their spouses, although they were unable to define it as husband rape. Others wrote letters about their children, who were crying from hunger. How could they stop it? Letter after letter to the BCS begged for answers to these questions.

It was to those letters that the BCS responded. Often these letters were written by women of British backgrounds, who were fluent in English. But it took little imagination on the part of the BCS women to realize the situation could hardly be better, and was no doubt worse, for women from different backgrounds.

The need became ever greater as word got out that there was an alternative for women, that women could have a *choice* in the matter. Lou's anger increased with the increased calls for help. The group, as always, had precious little money and their fundraising efforts never brought in enough. At meetings she began to rest eyes filled with accusation on the women with the wealthiest husbands. Why couldn't those ladies persuade their husbands to give more generously? Lou had done what she could with Jake.

But then Lou began to really look at those women. She noticed the lines of fatigue scrawled all over their faces, signs of sleepless nights and busy days. They gave in time, those women, what their husbands refused to give in money.

So Lou came up with an idea for fundraising. They should press the federal government for money, she thought, for health programs to meet women's needs for birth control and for classes on sex education at the school age level.

When she mentioned her idea to the others, however, it met with opposition. After all, the government was supplying them with a meeting place.

"That's the very least they can do," Lou replied. Her anger made her bold. She spoke to the other women about how she felt the government was using them to do the dirty work but putting forward nothing in the way of money or other support. If the government had moral reasons for supporting birth control, they would be willing to help meet the group's needs.

And besides, Lou continued, as long as women were working their fingers to the bone on the matter of birth control, the politicians didn't have to worry about any of them getting the notion to run for public office. Addressing the issue of birth control in the legislature might make the ladies think that social issues should always be of utmost concern to the members. And with things heating up in Europe, the honourable gentlemen in government probably reasoned, they must not steer off their path in preparing for battle.

Lou's reasoning provoked a reaction from many of the BCS members. After all, half of their husbands were in government, or connected to it in some way. "My dear, Louvina," they responded, "we don't want to do anything rash."

After Lou got home from that night's meeting, she sat down at the kitchen table and wrote angry letters to the government and the newspapers. It was clear the BCS would not back her ideas, let alone discuss them with the people in power.

Then, something else happened that made Lou re-examine her commitment to the BCS, and made her question if the BCS was always, in fact, doing what they thought they were doing—although she never doubted that the group did indeed help many, many women.

One Sunday, as was their habit every two months or so, Jake and Lou went to Winnipeg Beach to visit some old friends. Lou, true to the cause, took some Birth Control pamphlets with her. Despite any differences she had with the other BCS members, she was still dedicated to the idea of spreading the word on birth control.

The summer day had turned beautiful and sunny by the time they arrived at Winnipeg Beach. Lou and Jake and their friends decided to pack a picnic lunch and spend the afternoon by the lake. Their friends thought it would be nice to invite the local school teacher, Violet McPherson, to accompany them.

So as Jake and the other men went into the lake for a swim, Lou saw an opportunity to spread the word on birth control. She took the pamphlets out of her purse. Had Miss McPherson seen the latest information on birth control? No, she had not, Miss McPherson replied from under the brim of her straw hat. Lou pressed on: Miss McPherson was not instructing her older students in this important matter?

"No, there just aren't enough hours in the day," replied Miss McPherson. But, from out of her little velvet clutch purse, Miss McPherson pulled a pair of silver-rimmed spectacles. She read the pamphlet as she munched on a sandwich.

Then she folded the pamphlet against the skirt of her pale green dress, sighed and looked across at Lou, who sat on the other end of the flowered blanket.

For a moment, it seemed as if Miss McPherson was about to apologize to Lou. Certainly, she was struggling with her thoughts before she decided to speak her mind.

"I'm preparing two of my students for their Normal School entrance examinations," she said. "And, then, in the evenings, there's the tutoring."

"The tutoring?" queried Lou.

"Yes, young Johnny Chorcynski."

"Oh, you mean the Chorcynski family who lives down on the other end by the lake front? They fish, don't they?"

"Yes. Johnny is the son of Ted Chorcynski, who is the oldest member of that family. He married Olga Slawchuk."

Yes, Lou knew the woman and had met her more than once.

"Well, she was a bright girl," the teacher continued, "when she was in school. She enjoyed book reading and wrote poetry. She recited some of it at Christmas one year. In both English and Ukrainian, mind you, so her parents would understand it, too. Brought tears to her mother's eyes."

It turned out that Olga had gone on to have three children. But the third had been born with a withered hand. There was a lot of nonsense going around in the family that it was the mark of the devil but Miss McPherson told Olga not to believe a word of it. The teacher had soon realized that this child, a boy, was of above-average intelligence.

Olga had then begged the teacher to help her and the boy. The father had shunned his son. He thought the boy would amount to little with only one good hand. He could never fish, could he?

And somehow, Olga had told the teacher, she had been blamed for the boy's deformity because she had been very sick when she was pregnant with him. Now the elder Chorcynski was agreeing with the public health nurse, who said there were homes for types such as their son—homes for the mentally defective.

But Olga was determined to stand firm. She saw nothing wrong with her son's brains—and so what, even if there was? He was her son. She had not gone through that sickness during her pregnancy just to have him taken away from her.

"Oh, Miss McPherson, you should hear the poems he makes up out of his own little head," Olga had told the teacher. Olga said she would go along with the public health nurse, who had advised her to use birth control so as not to have another child like him. She did want more children, but she would not have her son taken away from her. He made her happy.

Writing poetry, Miss McPherson had replied, was all well and good but one must do something with one's life. She had suggested that Olga bring the boy to her house the following evening and she would see what could be done to help him. And Miss McPherson had worked with the boy several nights a week ever since, and was under the impression that he would someday be a lawyer.

Miss McPherson finished her story in a hoarse, conspiratorial whisper, as if speaking her hopes for the child too loudly might alert her opponents and they would condemn her plans for the boy long before they came to fruition. Lou noticed then, for the first time, that the teacher's eyes were very blue and very determined.

"I do believe people will have one Miss Violet McPherson to contend with if they decide to keep the lad from studying law because of his Ukrainian background or his withered hand," Lou laughed, after recounting the story to Jake on the way back to the city late that Sunday evening.

As their old jeep travelled past the evergreen trees, swamps and golden wheat fields, Lou's thoughts combed over the reason Miss Violet McPherson had been prompted to tell the story in the first place. What if the public health nurses had somehow known, before Johnny's birth, that he would have a withered hand? Lou wondered if Olga would have been allowed to make up her own mind about his birth. Certainly the nurse had done her utmost to control Olga's reproduction, against Olga's own preferences.

The teacher had given the name of the public health nurse to Lou, and Lou discovered that this nurse was endorsed by the BCS. So she relayed Miss McPherson's story to the other members. She suggested that the group had stepped far from its line of duty when it judged who was fit to have children and who was not. The BCS should, instead, be concentrating solely on distributing contraceptives to the women who were begging for them and had obviously made their own decisions about birth control. As it was, the BCS could barely cope with those numbers.

But, to Lou's surprise, more than one woman on the board did not share her views. After thinking things over during the sleepless night that followed the meeting, Lou went through much of the literature that had been distributed at BCS meetings.

There was material from the Toronto League for Race Betterment and it advocated reducing "mental defects" through birth control. This term took in a whole gamut of "abnormalities." In fact, the Mr. A.R. Kaufman who was held in such high regard by the members bandied around terms like "dull normal," and "careless, slovenly parents," and advocated the sterilization of such people because, he said, they were unable to use other forms of birth control. And, Lou discovered, he was instrumental in putting his philosophy into practice. The prejudice in his literature was vicious. For Lou, there was altogether too much talk about Science and nothing written from the heart.

As Lou sat behind the store counter that morning with this material spread out before her, she asked herself many questions that somehow had not come to mind earlier: How do you define "dull normal?" Were these people from an impoverished background, people who had simply never had access to education? Or perhaps they did not speak the King's English? And what about "careless" and "slovenly?" Perhaps they were too exhausted to seem bright and chipper at the end of an extremely long work day. To be sure, Kaufman saw fit to employ these "mental defectives," at dirt cheap wages, in his rubber company. They could contribute to society in that way.

Kaufman believed that sterilization of the "mentally defective" was preferable to locking them up in institutions. But Lou could not agree that these were the only options. And who had the right to play God?

Lou asked Jake that very question when he returned from making the morning deliveries. For centuries the Church had not allowed women to control their ability to conceive children. Now these men, with their Social Darwinism and "race betterment," were saying only a select group of superior beings, defined by them, should have children.

In spite of all this, Lou did not quit working for the BCS in the 1930s. She stayed, not to help those who believed in natural selection but to provide a path for women who decided, for themselves, not to have children, or to limit the number of children they did have. Her life experience had taught her that this was what she must do, but for the reasons in which she believed.

I will never know for sure if Lou intended to tell me more of her story, more of her ideas. When we parted on that last Monday, after we had shared lunch together in a cafe around the corner from my office, she gave me a hug. Then she turned and marched off to the bus stop, in her familiar, purposeful manner. She had never hugged me before.

Over the weekend, there was a spring blizzard. It was one of those storms no one expects until it happens. Then everyone remembers other years when the snow has melted and the winter boots have been put away, only in time to have a storm sweep through once more.

On Monday, I got ready for my appointment with Lou. A half-hour went by, and she still hadn't arrived. It was not like her to be late.

Another half-hour went by before I phoned her place. Her son answered. She had gone for a walk in the storm and had disappeared.

Three days later, they found Lou's body in a field north of the city. She had frozen to death.

I went around like an automaton for the next few days. I couldn't cry because I would not believe that this woman who had shared her story with me was not coming back.

On Friday, I came home tired, as usual, from a week's work and lay down on the couch for a nap.

I woke suddenly and said out loud to myself. "It's alright. I have her story."

Then, in relief, I cried.

TARA

I write Lou's story until mid-morning. Then I
sleep.

We are in a circle, the five of us around an open fire in a field in
a leftover world. I stand up. Walk quickly over to Lou. Her blood
washes over me and stops me from bleeding.

She is silent but I am speaking now in her voice.

Lou's bleeding stops. In the distance a baby cries. Lou closes
her eyes. Her body is still. She sighs out one final breath.

The other women go on bleeding. They look at me as if I am
a stranger. Juanita has fear in her eyes. Rita is angry. Miriam is
sad.

I do not hear their voices.

I wake to the sound of shuffling at my door, followed by the tap
of shoes going down the stairway outside my flat. I get up
quickly and rush to the door. There is a letter on the floor, left
there by my landlord. I see that it is from Miriam.

I decide I need to get out into the sunshine. I shove the letter
into my straw handbag and rush downstairs, over to the outdoor
cafe across the street. I order a glass of white wine, sip on it and
open the letter.

It is hurriedly written in Miriam's scrawl. She asks when I
will be coming home.

Good question. My ticket is open-ended. I have been here
two months already. Now that I am finally beginning to write

something it would be crazy to leave. This is why I have come here, after all: to write. This is why I quit my job at Women for Equality, took all my savings, put them into traveller's cheques and came to this island.

... At Women for Equality, we' re feeling deserted without you. Miriam writes. *Melda swears she would give up being on staff and give your job back if you came back. Our media contacts always ask for you. Everyone phones and asks for you. What are you doing over there, anyway?*

I get up and dash inside to the bar. Grab a postcard off the rack on the counter. Rush back out, digging in my handbag for a pen. My hand is shaking as I write across the back of the card: *I'M WRITING.*

I cross this out as I think of a better message: *I'M WRITING YOUR DAMN STORY.*

I breathe in and out a few times. Calm down. Sit down. Carefully, I write Miriam's address on the right hand side of the postcard. I pull a stamp out of the change purse in my bag, lick it and place it on the card.

I leave money on the table, including a nice tip, walk up to the corner and drop the postcard in a mailbox.

I turn and stride back to my flat. In no time, I am writing again. This, I realize as I get through the first page of Miriam's story, is the first time I have ever been angry at Miriam. Strangely, it feels good.

MIRIAM

Of all the women I know through Women for Equality, Miriam has so far been the only one who keeps in regular touch with me while I'm here on the island.

She is a small woman, but small in almost a delicate way. Her eyes are very unusual—iridescent. Her hair is black and clipped fairly close to her head. She always dresses with care.

Miriam is a medical doctor, and practises with two male physicians in the Tuxedo area of Winnipeg. Her clients are the people with new money, the people you see jogging in the late afternoons through Assiniboine Park. They like to get every ache and pain checked out.

So, like most doctors in Canada, she makes fistfuls of money although, in her case, she works only half-time. She chooses to live in an apartment building owned cooperatively by its residents so she can donate large chunks of her earnings to women's groups. These donations have always included Women for Equality.

We got to know each other well and to like each other well because of our involvement in feminist activism. We planned many demonstrations, discussed strategy at numerous meetings and raised hell together on many occasions. To coax and cajole the establishment into seeing things our way was important to us both. And, enjoyable. Very enjoyable.

I first worked with Miriam shortly after I started with Women for Equality. A new provincial government had been elected and, at the first board meeting I attended, it was decided that a couple of us should try to set up a meeting with the new premier.

Miriam and I took on the project. We managed to set a date

for the meeting after making several phone calls to respective MLAs, assistants to the premier, assistants to the minister and so on. This accomplished, we decided to get together for an evening brainstorm and sort out which issues to set as our priorities when talking with the politicians.

Miriam suggested we meet at her apartment—it would be nicer for an evening meeting than the office. I agreed and arrived at her place right after supper.

She answered the door with what I thought, at first, was a dog by her legs. Then, as it turned to rush from me at the door, I noticed its bushy tail. It was a red fox.

I must have shown my surprise.

"Oh, I forgot to tell you about Ruby," Miriam said. "Sometimes people prefer to be warned ahead of time about her."

The fox had returned to stand in the hall. Her narrow eyes glared at me coldly.

"I have a bit of a farm up near Gimli," Miriam went on. "I've collected a rather unusual assortment of animals and they stay around my cabin up there. You can't really call it a farm, but a farmer in the area drops by to feed them every day. I get out there once a week to visit them. More often when the weather's nice.

"Every so often," she continued, "I bring one or the other of them into the city to stay for a spell. One at a time, of course. My apartment isn't big enough for more than one at a time. So, don't worry, you won't run into any others."

I thought this was a little kooky. But I was glad, too. I liked Miriam from that moment on.

She showed me into a small sitting room, and while she went into another room to take care of the fox, I took a look around me.

The floor had thick, light brown carpet. The couch and armchairs were goldish-green. The pink brick fireplace had wood already laid in it—to be lit later in the evening, I guessed. The drapes were chocolate-brown, and were drawn. A table by each armchair displayed an antique lamp. Both were ... I was going to write "lit," but they did, of course, run on electricity. The warmth in that room was palpable.

Finally, my eyes were drawn to the wall above the plump couch, where three wide brown oval frames hung one below the other and each to the right of the one above it. In each frame was a portrait of a woman with short dark hair and Miriam's eyes, those beautiful iridescent eyes.

They all could have been portraits of Miriam, but I thought not. Something was slightly different about each woman. The one on the top had a parasol tilted over one shoulder. The middle one had a kerchief tied around her neck. The one on the bottom had hair even shorter than the other two.

But differences such as those are nothing. One woman can change her hairstyle or carry an accessory, like a parasol, from the past. No, it was something akin to the warmth I felt in the room. Each woman contributed something different, although they were so close to being the same. I could sense this in a way I can't quite explain.

It was when Miriam spoke from directly behind me that I realized she was back in the room. "The first one is my grandmother. The middle one, my mother. I'm the third," she said.

"I want to know them," I said, impulsively. "I mean, I want to know their stories ... your stories."

Miriam did not seem taken aback by this statement. We sat down and did our business together. Then Miriam brought a glass of white wine for each of us. The fox came in and curled by my feet. She told me two strangely beautiful stories, one for each portrait except her own.

Miriam's grandmother crossed over from England in Miriam's great-grandmother's womb, sometime during the 1880s. The pregnant woman never had so much as a headache on the entire voyage, but most other passengers were violently ill. She cared for the sick and saved many lives.

Miriam was told that her great-grandmother was into her eleventh month of carrying the baby when she finally gave birth. It was said that she had willed her child to remain safe inside her until the family was settled into two upstairs rooms in Winnipeg. These rooms were to remain home for several years.

Miriam's great-grandfather took a job in a horse stable. He set aside a large portion of his earnings towards paying for the grain he planned to plant on the land allotted him by the Canadian government. Miriam's great-grandmother nurtured one child after another after another, and she cooked and cleaned and mended—all those extraordinary things women with families did.

Sarah, Miriam's grandmother, had an ordinary enough childhood. She married in her early teens and showed every sign of following in her mother's footsteps. Her husband bought the horse stables from her father, who had never quite managed to get the money he needed to start farming. Sarah and her husband moved into two rooms above an apothecary shop on Main Street and Sarah became pregnant almost immediately.

But Sarah's life took a more interesting turn when she met and befriended a woman named Emily. Emily boarded in a rooming house next door and worked as a governess for a wealthy land developer who lived, with his children, further north on Main Street.

Together the two would go out on moonlit nights to wander across the prairies. In those days, Winnipeg's windy Main Street lost itself in the wheatfields and unbroken grasslands to the west, and hugged the Red River on its east.

The neighbours spied the two women, of course, as they strolled out, arm-in-arm, onto the land. There was talk. How could Sarah's husband allow her to venture out into the wilds like that? What kind of man was he, anyway?

But such gossip and condemnation did not command the full attention of the neighbours, because there was another matter for them to discuss. This matter concerned the wealthy land developer who employed Emily.

This land developer's mansion was built of stone, and surrounded by a stone fence, which enclosed an English garden and a fish pond. Passers-by noticed this house. They also noticed, as they strolled by in the evenings, the blood-curdling screams that would issue out of the house.

Most people believed the screams were connected with the ghost of the woman who had married the land developer. In their life together, it was said, he ruled over her as a lord does over his servant or slave. "Poor soul, she cannot rest in peace from his tormenting her even yet," people would agree quietly among themselves when the subject came up.

Having solved the mystery of the mansion the neighbours again turned their attention to wondering why Sarah's husband allowed her to wander her nights away with Emily.

One night, people had their curiosities on both matters piqued. The land developer was struck down by a heart attack. His gardener, who lived on the grounds, found his master staggering among the hollyhocks, his hand clutched to his chest while he mouthed curses.

The gardener raced down the street, attracting others who joined him as he rushed up the stairs to Sarah's husband's room. The idea was to get a horse from the stable and ride out for the doctor, who was attending a patient at one of the homesteads.

Sarah's husband was so deep in sleep that it took the gardener several minutes to shake him awake. By the bed, on a night table, were the remains of a warm glass of milk. The gardener sniffed it and smelled rum.

From that night on, word spread that Sarah served her husband a toddy on the nights she wanted him to sleep especially sound so that she could go out on her strolls with Emily. Some said he did not know the substance he drank was rum—although that is hard to believe.

In the meantime, the men shook the stable owner awake. When the horse was saddled up and the doctor sent for, Miriam's grandfather turned his attentions back to his missing wife. Someone was quick to instruct him as to the probable whereabouts of Sarah.

So, out he trooped onto the prairies—with all but one of his children in tow, for he did not want harm to come to them while he was away from home. Ruth, the seventh and the youngest, was missing, until they found her with Sarah and Emily, sleeping near an open fire they had built.

Miriam did not say what her grandfather's reaction was, but she did tell me what Ruth, who was Miriam's mother, had seen Sarah and Emily do that evening. They had hauled clay up from the banks of the Red River. They had made two figures. One was the figure of a man, and the other was of a woman. They had hollowed out the crotch of the female figure, so that she appeared to be mutilated there.

As the figure's clay hardened near the fire, blue welts appeared all over her body. Sarah and Emily placed a pointed stick in the chest of the male image, and rust-coloured fluid gushed from the wound. Ruth told Miriam that she did not know what the fluid was—it could have been merely some water from the river mixed with clay.

Long after Sarah's death, Miriam was going through boxes of her grandmother's things in her mother's attic when she found a book, a diary. It served to pull together the loose ends of the story.

In the little book—a diary with purple violets on the cover— a woman wrote about the horrors of being raped over and over again by her father, a wealthy land dealer. She told of violence towards her that began shortly after the death of the man's wife, her mother.

She believed that the devil had entered him. She wrote of his feet turning into hooves. They would kick deep blue bruises into her body while he "lashed" into her.

She seemed terrified that her governess, whom she "loved with all her heart and soul," would discover her diary and the terrible secret she shared with her father. She feared that her governess would know how bad she was and desert her forever. The townspeople would know of her father's affliction and would condemn her, too, for leading this "well-respected" man to become the devil. The woman was terrified of all these things, and yet she had the strength to write them down.

Ruth, Miriam's mother, bore Miriam late in life. Ruth was already in her forties and there was a wide gap in age between this youngest child and her six other children. She had almost given up the hope of having a seventh child when she found herself pregnant with Miriam—who was to become the seventh born to the seventh born. Indeed, Ruth believed that this made Miriam nothing short of magical. Her daughter, she was sure, would carry on the much-needed work that she had begun.

To describe the kind of work done by Ruth (and later by Miriam) is a difficult thing. Like anything else rooted in spirituality, one has to believe in it and have faith. If Ruth had been a doctor, it would be easier to explain in terms we can readily understand—or think we understand. But Ruth cannot be pinned down in that way. Perhaps it is best to tell the story as Miriam tells it, and leave it at that.

Miriam, from very early on in life, knew that the brooch her mother constantly wore somehow symbolized, or was part of, the work she did. The brooch had been given to Ruth by her husband shortly after they were married. It was an unusual piece of jewellery, in the shape of a black snake with an iridescent eye. Obviously that jewel of an eye, which matched Ruth's eyes, had prompted Miriam's father to buy the brooch.

Miriam's father was a gambler and when he had money he spent it on gifts, which he lavished upon Ruth. But often Miriam's father was only one step ahead of his debtors, which explains why the family lived generally in the North End but at no fixed address. Within the radius of a few miles, they seemed to be constantly moving from one suite of rooms to another. Ruth had insisted that her children should remain in the same school, in order to receive a solid education. So they had to stay in one area of the city. In this, Ruth was the typical mother—wanting the best for her children's future.

Otherwise, Ruth was far from what you might call a doting mother. She was in many ways still a child herself, and she loved to play. She adored dressing up in the beads and bangles of the 20s, while her husband donned the hats and suits of that era. Then they would party—sometimes with the wealthiest people in the city. Many of their friends were luckier at gambling and other shady deals than Ruth's husband was.

Oddly, however, Ruth used to tell her youngest child that for all their gaiety together she could count on two hands the number of times she and her husband had made love. She vowed this was why they had remained good friends for the thirty-odd years of their marriage.

Once, Miriam challenged her mother on this. "How can that be, Ruth?" Miriam asked, with the part of her that was the sceptical scientist. "You did have seven children, you know. That takes some doing."

"Not as much doing as you think," Ruth told her youngest. "Be open to unexplained energy. That is the key."

And while Miriam's father spent more and more of his nights in one backroom or another—anywhere a card game happened to be—Ruth's energies were free to go into other things.

Ruth played with cards, too—but she told fortunes with them. By day, she visited one parlour room after another in homes all over the city. Towards the end, in the 50s, Miriam would tag along with her mother. She remembered Ruth in flamboyant dress which changed from one day to the next, although she always wore the snake brooch. Ruth saw many things, good and bad, as she went to house after house.

The good did not concern Ruth. It was the bad that she acted upon, trying to change it. But she was not fighting for social justice or for women's rights and she definitely was not a "do-gooder." Something compelled her to right those wrongs. Things appeared literally out of place to Ruth, out of order, until the distressing situations she witnessed could be righted.

And Ruth couldn't force herself to stop. She wasn't an orderly housewife, she didn't care about order in material things. But she wanted people to be whole. If they were sick of spirit, she would want them to be well.

For instance, there was one woman whose palm Ruth would read at the end of each month. The woman worked doing dress alterations for a clothing shop, so she was able to give Ruth a "little something" for her trouble.

Miriam recalled going with her mother to the woman's place around four o'clock, just after the woman got back from taking her alterations to the shop and before her husband got home. It was important, Ruth knew, to get there before the husband got home from his job. If he were to catch his wife having her palm read, Ruth sensed that things would not go well for the woman. The woman had confided to Ruth that her husband did not like her to spend money on herself.

One particular day at the end of the month, it was very cold and Ruth wondered whether she should bother visiting this woman. In the end, she "felt" she should go, and she bundled up both Miriam and herself.

When they arrived at the woman's home, Ruth found the woman sick in bed. She was bleeding, her youngest daughter said, and had been doing so for almost two days. It was heavy bleeding. Miriam thought later it must have been a miscarriage. At the time, Ruth asked if there had been a doctor called in to take a look at her. No, the little girl replied, because her father did not believe his wife was sick—only lazy.

Ruth's face hardened with anger. Quickly, she went into the kitchen and put a kettle on to boil. From a pouch in one of her bags, she took out some herbs, which she brewed up like tea once the water had come to a boil. The woman drank and when the colour returned to her cheeks, Ruth left Miriam to watch over the sick woman while she herself fetched a doctor.

After Ruth returned with the doctor, Ruth and Miriam stayed on for several hours. The doctor examined the woman and left some medicine, for which Ruth paid out of her own slim purse. Then, she stayed awhile to make the woman as comfortable as possible. It had been dark for some time when they left that house.

As they were leaving, the husband arrived home. Ruth refused to say so much as "good evening" when they passed him at the door. But on the floor, in the porch near where they had left their boots spread out over pieces of the Saturday newspaper, Miriam spied a black snake slithering up into the house. Weeks later word reached Ruth that the husband had come down with an illness only a few days after she had helped save his wife's life. He was bleeding inside his guts and "sicker than a dog," people said. Miriam got the impression he was close to death.

Months later, Ruth and Miriam ran into the couple, with their daughter, in the park. They were walking arm-in-arm. Miriam could hardly believe what she was seeing. The harsh man she had seen arriving home with the smell of liquor about him as his wife lay sick, seemed to have a gentleness about him now. His rounded shoulders under a brown sweater made him seem soft somehow.

Miriam glanced up at her mother, and saw a smile on her lips.

Soon after that, Miriam and Ruth worked telling fortunes at a fair. Ruth read cards in one of the booths and Miriam sat with her, the little helper who ran for cool drinks when her mother was thirsty, or stayed to turn cards over for a customer.

Next to their booth was a pony ride, where a scruffy little animal, with matted hair and tied to the end of a rope, walked round and round a red-and-white striped pole. Sometime during their second day there, Miriam realized the animal did not want to be there. She saw his big bloodshot eyes and his slow plodding movements as being what they were—signs of his suffering.

All day long, the young man who owned the pony ride barked at the people as they went by. Parents thought it would be cute to see their children on the back of the small beast, and some of the kids begged their parents for a ride.

Towards the end of the second afternoon, a huge man rumbled up to the pony ride. Miriam remembered he wore a cowboy hat and a wide black belt with a silver buckle on it. He shoved a dollar bill into the hand of the pony owner. The young man shook his head. "It's only for kids," he said. The big man shoved another bill into his hand. "Okay," the owner nodded.

The big man was actually going to ride the pony, Miriam realized. Surely, it would hurt the animal even more than it was hurting already. Miriam looked up at her mother, and Ruth understood.

Suddenly, the animal made a break for it. He took off galloping, and it was truly amazing the way that tired, worn-out little animal ran, kicking up dust as he left. The broken rope, trailing from his neck, was like a grey snake darting after him. Miriam looked up at her mother. Ruth was holding her hand over her brooch.

The young man cursed as he held up the other end of the rope where it had, it seemed, frayed close to the pole and finally broken off. The giant yelled for his money back.

It wasn't until that fall that a man who lived on the west end of Selkirk Avenue discovered the pony near an enclosed field where he kept his own horse. The pony had been attracted by the oats the man put out for his horse each day. With the fair long gone and the young man with it, no one cared to do anything about the pony. It kept close to the horse for the winter and left in the spring.

Miriam told one more story about her mother. Ruth had befriended a prostitute called Rose. Actually, Miriam's father knew Rose first, for she frequented the gambling rooms where he spent a lot of his time. She was usually either plying her trade or gambling away her earnings.

Rose's dream was to be so lucky at gambling, to hit such a big jackpot, that she would never again have to sell her body. When Ruth's husband brought Rose back to their rooms one night, she was very thin and obviously needed to eat some good food. And Ruth cooked for this woman, although cooking was something she seldom did for anyone.

Rose had been gambling steadily for several days. She had been on a winning streak and thought that this time, for sure, she would win her way out of prostitution. For the last couple of days, she hadn't even stopped to eat. Then she lost all her money and, as if that weren't enough, she lost it to one of her regular customers.

Rose and this man had a strange relationship. He was an alcoholic and a glutton, and he never washed his hair or body. But he was a lawyer, and was loaded with money. If you looked up his address in the phone book, you would find he lived in wealthy River Heights. His wife was a homemaker, a good, self-effacing person who cared for their two sons.

The lawyer often told people at parties, in a grating voice, about how he was leaving half of all his worldly goods to Rose when he died. On the night Ruth met Rose, she had lost every cent gambling against him. Because he didn't want to be deprived of Rose's services for the rest of his life, he had played against her and won her earnings. It was after that incident that Ruth became involved, and a few months later the lawyer died, of a rare disease. Rose wore black to the reading of his will and retired to Hawaii shortly after.

When Ruth died, she went quickly. Her hair turned completely white, literally overnight. Her energy left her and Miriam felt a surge of vitality enter into her own body.

On the morning Miriam and I were to meet with the premier, I dressed carefully. I put on my dark-blue suit: an A-line dress with a short, matching jacket. My pantyhose and low-heeled shoes were a matching navy-blue. I even pulled my briefcase out of the closet for the occasion.

When I met Miriam, as arranged, near the statue of the bison in the front lobby of the legislative building, I noticed she had taken even greater care than I had in dressing for the occasion.

She wore a tunic-style black jacket that fit loosely over a white blouse. A tie was done up in a fairly large bow at the collar. Her skirt was black and pleated. Her pantyhose and shoes were black as well.

But it was the brooch on her lapel that made me comment. "Oh, that must be it," I said. And there it was: the black snake outlined in silver, with its large eye. The eye glinted with exactly the same iridescence as Miriam's eyes. It took energy, on my part, to pull my eyes away from it.

We had quite a long wait before we saw the premier. Some minor scandal—a married cabinet minister caught having an affair with one of his unmarried aides—had prompted an unscheduled press conference for the premier. His secretary assured us that the premier would see us the moment he was through with the press.

We waited and drank coffee. We drank coffee and waited.

Finally, we were shown into the office. The premier rose from a dark brown armchair and greeted us as we walked in. He was a nondescript man—sort of balding, sort of greying, sort of tall, sort of flabby. He was flanked by a female assistant, whom I recognized as someone who had been active in the Status of Women groups of the teachers' society. I remembered her face from the evening television news.

After coffee was set out and everyone had taken what they wanted from the silver cream and sugar bowls, we began our pitch to the premier. We outlined the need for more education in the schools that specifically condemned violence against women. We expressed our desire to encourage teachers to eliminate sex role stereotyping. We went on to articulate the situation women face after men rape or batter them. We talked about women being raped again by the justice system. We told the premier about women unable to gain economic independence from their batterers because of unemployment, and this led us into our discussion about the violence of economic poverty.

At first, the premier responded by telling us an "anecdote" about his neighbour's son who, at five years old, was hitting a little girl while they waited for the school bus.

I held back my temper. Miriam and I had agreed beforehand not to express our anger, no matter how much the premier trivialized what we were trying to tell him.

Then, something happened. The premier's manner changed completely. He began promising to pass legislation "with teeth in it" based on what we had told him. He had his aide taking notes left, right and centre.

I couldn't believe it. In my astonishment, I looked over at Miriam. She was stroking something in the palm of her hand.

Her brooch.

It was no longer on the lapel of her jacket; and its eye was glittering when Miriam opened her hand for me to see.

TARA

I finally take a break from the typewriter when I feel my legs falling asleep. I get up, go to the fridge and pull out a bottle of white grape juice, pour it into a glass and gulp it down. I was thirsty, I realize.

I move out onto the balcony. The sun is a deep orange ball in the sky. If I hurry, I will get down to the sea before it pulls itself behind the stone fort.

I go back inside, throw on my jean jacket and grab my bag. I am out, down the hill and walking along the harbour in no time but still the sun's fire is gone by the time I reach the cafes and pubs at the docks near the fort.

I stop to button up my jacket. There is a cool breeze blowing off the sea. I look out and up. I inhale, through all five of my senses, the navy-blue sky with its fields of stars.

"Hello." A man has come out of nowhere as they always do on this island. I turn quickly and head towards the light. I end up in the doorway of a shop displaying intricately handmade, off-white lace doilies and tacky commercial souvenirs— placemats and pelicans on rocks. Near the entrance is a rack of porn magazines mixed in with the daily newspapers. I buy an English language paper and go next door to eat dinner in a pub.

A waiter comes with a laminated menu. I immediately decide to have moussaka. After ordering, I open the paper. It's still early and the place is deserted but I am not taking any chances. Reading, I hope, will be a signal that I am not looking for company.

A photograph on the left hand side of an article grabs my attention. Most of the women in the picture do not look any different from the Greek Cypriot women I see every day here. The older ones are in dark dress with kerchiefs on their heads. The younger ones wear loosely curled shoulder-length hair, sweaters over blouses and dark skirts, stockings and shoes.

But in the middle of this group of women, who are mostly squatting on the ground or sitting politely with legs curled together and under the body, rises one woman, like Artemis, from their midst.

I recognize the woman but can't place her. She has long, thick hair and huge beautiful eyes that even the black-and-white photo cannot hide. Tall and slender, she wears a short, tailored blazer and pants. I look more closely. They might even be blue jeans. If they are, this is the first Greek Cypriot woman I have seen in jeans during my time on the island. The news story informs me that the woman is a spokesperson for hundreds, thousands of women, who are demanding a return to their homes.

The whole story is not a simple one. My lover Nikos has tried to explain it to me: in Cyprus, the woman often determines where her husband and family live. A young man moves into his new wife's home after marriage. It is the woman's lineage that links the past with the future. This, I get the impression, is the woman's power in a culture where men most definitely have the edge when it comes to everything else.

The island lives under an uneasy ceasefire after a long war between the Turkish and Greek peoples. It has taken away from the island's daughters the little power they had. Their homes and their villages have been in their bloodlines since ancient times. But not anymore. The war has pushed the Greek women, along with their families, into the south.

They end up in refugee villages in the south. The Turkish Cypriots, who were forced by the Greeks into the north, live in similar villages far from their homes in the south.

War is a two-way street. A village for a village. An eye for an eye. A son for a son. A grave for a grave. The women bury their sons one day and are herded out of their homes the next.

On the next page, I see other photos of all those women standing at the wire fences near Famagusta where the Turkish army is occupying the island. The women look like beggars being barred from the palace gates. Beggars in their own land. Refugees in their own land.

I am tempted to go and join them.

In some ways, my nightmare has turned into a dream. The bleeding wounds have stopped. On the other hand, nothing else has really changed. I can hear Lou's voice but I cannot hear what the other women are saying. They can't hear each other. No one else can hear them.

I wake up frustrated.

Next morning, Nikos comes by and we go for a ride along the Mediterranean. When he drops me off around noon, I find a postcard left on my doormat. It bears the University of Winnipeg insignia so I know it must be from Rita, who teaches there. With a start, I realize the spokeswoman in yesterday's newspaper photo reminds me of Rita.

I turn over the card. The message reads: *WHY AREN'T YOU WRITING YOUR OWN GODDAMN STORY? Love, Rita.*

So they have been talking about me, Miriam and Rita. Deciding, as usual, what it is I should be doing instead of trusting me to do the right thing.

I dig in a cupboard drawer, find a postcard and quickly write across the back: *Dear Rita, Who do you think is going to write down your stories if I don't? What would have happened to Lou's story if I hadn't taken the time to come over here and write it? You're an historian. Why do you have such little value for the past?*

I cast my mind back to when the green scribbler had sat in my desk drawer for months, and I had approached the Women for Equality board with my idea. I wanted to take the summer to write those stories down. Maybe I'd even have them ready to submit to a publisher in the fall. Summer wasn't busy and I had loads of overtime coming to me.

The answer was an absolute "no." Rita was the most vocal opponent. I should be preparing a brief for the upcoming changes to the sexual assault laws in the fall. I should be supervising the summer students. I should be organizing rallies against the porn shops.

"Why are you doing this anyway?" Rita asked me. "Surely, you don't think the stories are more important than the sexual assault laws?"

"Not *more* important but *as* important," I said.

Rita's laugh sounded like a snort. "Why?"

I couldn't answer.

"Why don't you write your own story? What about that, eh?"

I couldn't answer.

"Eh?"

"Are you saying I can't work on your stories?" I asked.

Rita looked at me. "No, I trust you with them, if that's what you mean. But not on our time. Women for Equality has more important work to do."

By fall, I had resigned. I took my savings and my green scribbler and was on an open-ended seat-sale flight to Cyprus: somewhere warm where I could write for the winter, or maybe even longer. I had no definite plans to return to Canada.

And maybe this is why the Greek Cypriot women in the newspaper would throw up their hands in disgust with me if they got to know me and found that I was halfway around the world from my home. My parent's home, they would say, is my home and I should be in it. "Okay, okay," they might say. "If you have to, then you could work outside your home but near your village, parakalo."

I wonder if the tall spokesperson, whom I have nicknamed Artemis, would think the same way. I am beginning to toy with the idea of taking a bus to where the women are. I could interview them. Somewhere back home a newspaper or magazine would be interested in their story.

Instead, though, I sit at my typewriter and begin to write about Rita. I know that, if the woman in the photograph really was Rita, she would articulate her anger immediately.

RITA

The first time I saw Rita, she was standing on a podium and she was speaking against the United States' military intervention in Central America.

It was at the International Women's Day March. The day was bitterly cold, one of those winter days in Winnipeg when the sun makes the snow sparkle but the climate can freeze noses and feet very quickly if you don't dress for it. Still, a fairly large crowd of staunch activists came out for the march, which ended at the legislative buildings on Broadway. Once there, we had speeches.

Most of them were quite boring, as I recall, but everyone had to have her say, whether politician or IWD Committee member, so we stood stamping our feet in an attempt to keep warm. The speakers droned on. We clapped (it kept the circulation in the hands going) and the next speaker was introduced.

As I looked around the crowd on the day of the march, I saw Juanita standing on the other side of the legislative building's front steps. She was dwarfed by a tall woman who wore a white parka and knitted hat. The clothes contrasted with her dark hair and eyes and served to make her stand out, as we huddled together for warmth.

Juanita spoke little at the IWD meetings, but one thing she insisted upon was that her professor-friend Rita should talk on behalf of the women struggling in Central America. When it was Rita's turn to speak this day, she strode up the steps to the microphone. She spoke with such passion about the struggles of the people in Central America that the foot stamping stopped for awhile. We listened to her.

After it was over and we finished things off with a few choruses of "Bread and Roses," I edged over to where Juanita and Rita were standing. I wanted to introduce myself to Juanita's friend. The three of us decided to hop a bus and go down to the Union Centre for some beer.

We wound up spending the rest of the afternoon and a good part of the evening at the Union Centre. Gradually, our conversation got past the carefully polite stages of not knowing each other and that is when I started asking Rita questions about her life.

Soon she was talking freely about it. She wanted to tell her story, Rita said, because each time she told it there was that much more of a chance that things would right themselves for women, and for her homeland, too.

As she talked and explained things to me, I found it interesting that she, unlike Juanita, came from a wealthy background. I also realized that she had an intensity about her ideals that Juanita did not have. Juanita was more relaxed. This surprised me at first, for I assumed that Juanita must have experienced many more hardships than Rita.

Over the weeks, I got to know Rita better. Our paths crossed when she joined the Violence Against Women Committee I formed through my job at Women For Equality. I found myself dropping something off at Rita's apartment and staying for cafe con leche. Often we would go out for a late dinner after evening meetings, and on a couple of occasions I had her over for supper. Her marriage and my live-in relationship were ending so we started to keep each other company on the weekends.

At one point, I showed her my green scribbler and said I would like to take some notes based on the stories she was telling me so that, when I had the time someday, I would be able to write about her. She more than welcomed the idea. Somehow I think it made her feel there was purpose to our getting together, to our friendship. Like me, Rita felt spending time not doing something for "the cause" was wasted time.

Rita, as I have mentioned already, was born into wealth, into the ruling class. She was the eldest daughter of Dr. Pedro Cortez, who was the eldest son of a large landowner. The family was entirely of Spanish descent. It was important to her grandfather and her father that the bloodline be kept pure.

So to avoid "contamination" (as Rita had been taught to call it), the Cortez children attended private schools. It was at these schools that Rita learned to master English, which she spoke fluently by the time I got to know her. Her school colours were not the navy or grey of the public school students. Instead, they were a distinctive gold and maroon. A person's colour of dress says a lot in Guatemala City.

Something else Rita recalled very distinctly from her childhood was the garden around which their mansion was built. It was (and probably still is) huge, filled with weeping willows and flowing vines covered in peach-coloured flowers.

In the centre of the large artificial pond was a water fountain. A soldier of hard marble stood erect as the water ran down the veins in his muscular arms and trickled to the bottom, where huge goldfish darted through the seaweeds or lay eggs among the pink and blue pebbles.

Around this pond strutted a stork, kept by Rita's mother as a pet. She had purchased it once in Spain during a family tour through Europe. On hot days, it would sometimes wade into the pond water and then, maybe because they were right under its stout beak, it would pick up one or two goldfish and leave them flopping until they died at the side of the pond. The bird had no desire to eat them, for Rita's mother had spoiled her pet with the finest caviar and other seafood delicacies.

When Rita was very small, she would be led out onto the balcony each day by the nurse. Once there, she would gaze down upon the family's personal Garden of Eden. If she looked up from the garden and directly across the complex, she could see her papa. He would be wearing a burgundy dressing gown and smoking his morning pipe. Often, in other corners of the balcony which ran along the four sides of the mansion, she would see brothers or sisters paying similar homage to their wealth as they gazed down upon the courtyard garden.

On many evenings, Rita's parents would throw parties in that garden. She recalled the military generals and generals' sons who lusted after her family's wealth and her beauty. There was talk of family unions between her father and the military, and she was the middle woman, the shiny ribbon that would tie the men together. Her body would be sacrificed for the union of powerful men. These things were assumed.

Rita played these evenings in the garden like a game. It was as if she was watching herself from the balcony seat in front of her suite of rooms. She would throw her head back, her long mane of hair flowing in the evening breeze as her white teeth flashed in the dusk.

She remembered one puffed-up young army man who had rushed up to her gallantly, to pull out her chair at the table as they were sitting down to dinner during one of the parties. By mistake, when he pulled out the chair, he placed it on his foot. Not knowing this, Rita sat down. The hero groaned in pain and unceremoniously pushed her off the chair. In the garden with the blue stork who fished but did not eat his prey, Rita learned much about the courage of the men sanctioned by the state to kill.

Rita learned about revolution in university. First, her brother, Altraz, encouraged her to attend the school, and then he selected for her a couple of leftist professors. He gave her books to read. He invited her to "hang out" with him and his lover, Lise, in the room they rented near the markets in the city centre. It was Lise who had led Altraz into radical politics. He had been training to be a doctor when he met her.

Rita remembered looking out of the narrow window in their rented room and onto the tin roofs of the clothing markets below. Everything that could be painted in the room was a sickly aqua-green colour, and greasy. Everything in that room—everything in the whole building—was sticky to the touch.

The room had nothing in it, other than a narrow bed covered with a grey blanket and an old wooden chair, its aqua-green paint peeling and the brown of an earlier coat of paint showing through.

If their plans were very private, then four or five of the student radicals would crowd into that room late at night. At other times, they would take their meals in the common room. The cook made greasy food and he, like everything else in the place, was dirty. His hair was dirty. His skin was oily. There was no hot water for showers or washing. Sometimes Rita would sneak out of her parents' house in the morning without taking a bath or washing her hair. She wanted to fit in with the others. Often she would leave with a shoulder pack of food to share with the comrades.

Each night Rita returned, often very late, to her parents' home. She bribed the servants to keep silent about her late returns. She knew her parents would refuse to allow her to go out if they found she was following in her older brother's footsteps.

Rita's father had disowned Altraz. As her father put it, Altraz fought for and even "fucked" the peasants. The old man would shake his head back and forth as he discussed these things with his wife late at night, in their rooms above the garden. He never mentioned his son to his friends in the military. One could not trust such men and he did not hate his eldest enough to promote his death. Coming as he did from the ruling class, Altraz would not be subjected to interrogations, torture and the firing squad. But, still, one never knew.

Altraz' father did not know how deep his son was into things. Altraz and Lise were closely associated with the poor farmers and the unions. Through this solidarity work, the two became linked with the Sandinistas in Nicaragua, before the Sandinistas gained control of the government from the dictator Somoza. They helped smuggle people through Guatemala on their way to the United States or Canada.

Rita became involved in this work. She saw the refugees as they came through. At first, they were mostly labour leaders, known leftists. Then, there were other workers, farmers, peasants, even some priests and sisters. Of course, many more—most—stayed in their homeland. They stayed and fought and were maimed and died for the revolution. The ones Rita met were running for their lives. They were sweating fear. It was a most sickly-sour smell, Rita told me, this smell of terror.

Rita told me of one woman, in particular. This woman had been in the habit of taking a walk in the woods after her large family were all in bed. This habit both saved her life, and made her wish her life had ended.

The woman's husband laboured in the fields, on land owned by a large company. He hated his work, save for the contact it gave him with other workers, other men whose fathers had owned their own land but had finally been forced to sell to the company. Who could compete with the company?

After years of preaching to his brothers about the corruption of the large landowners, this man decided he could do something about it. Elections were coming up. The mayor, a puppet of the company, was running for re-election. It was to be his fifth term. No one ever ran against him, although few citizens seemed to benefit from his being in office. And after each re-election the mayor pulled out his belt another notch to accommodate his expanding midriff.

On this particular year, the woman's husband made up his mind to challenge the mayor. He printed up handbills and distributed them around the town: in the bars, to the farm labourers, in the market place. Every night, he would go down to the town square and talk with the other cooperatives. He wondered aloud as to why the mayor had the only running water in the town. The people nodded their heads—they worked hard, really hard, for nothing.

Often, the woman worked even harder than her husband. True, she had the smiling faces of her children to thank her, but still her chores were endless. I won't bore you with a list of women's work in the home, but such work kept her and other women out of politics. She knew only that her husband was going against the grain. She seldom went down to the town square, and she couldn't read the handbills or anything else. At night she got her children ready for sleep and put them to bed. She made love to her husband and stroked his aching back until he fell asleep. Then an hour was hers. She walked out into the night, with the stars and the night birds and the trees. The breeze seemed to bind them all together.

In due course, election day arrived. This woman's husband did not win, of course—it was a simple matter to rig the ballot box. But he had won the support of the people. Some people actually thought they should have some say about their work in the fields owned by the multinational company. There was talk of a union representative, who would visit the area.

One night, six weeks after the election, the woman returned from her nightly walk. She felt a bit chilly so she crawled quickly into bed and reached over to borrow some warmth from her husband. He was as cold as ice. Her eyes adjusted to the dark and she noticed a knife sticking out of his belly. She backed out of the bed in horror. Out of long habit, she went to the crib to check her baby. Her head was bent back, her neck broken. All of her six children had suffered the same fate, she soon found. She heard a rustling in the house, and she ran.

When Rita met her a few days later, the woman seemed as if she was in a trance. She had been shunted quickly from one comrade to another and was being propelled towards Canada. She could not speak English but, she was told, she would be safe there. If anyone was able to qualify for refugee status, it would be someone with a horror story like hers.

Altraz brought the woman to Rita at the cafe on the university campus. There was no way someone would be ready to help her across the border until the next day. Altraz was concerned because the woman was completely withdrawn, hadn't said a word since her arrival. Would Rita take her home? Rita had done this before. The mansion was huge, and her parents and siblings seldom ventured into her suite of rooms. The servants were on her side when it came to helping these people. She had taken the two most trustworthy servants into her confidence and they would act as assistants and look-outs when she brought someone to the house.

Rita settled this particular woman into bed and ordered some dinner for her. The woman had remained mute on the car ride home and showed no signs of opening up. Rita thought the woman might feel better after sleeping and eating, so she left to read in an adjoining room.

A few minutes later, Rita heard the woman cry out. She ran into the bedroom and found her weeping uncontrollably. The woman, who was fumbling at her throat while she cried, was twice Rita's age (Rita was eighteen) but she obviously needed to be comforted. So Rita gathered the woman into her arms.

The woman was upset because she had lost a locket that she had always worn around her neck. In the locket was a photo of one of her daughters. Now, the only connection she had with the past was gone. The woman poured out her story as she clutched at Rita's clothing.

Above all else, the woman wanted to know why her family had been slain. It was not a philosophical question. She merely was not able to connect her husband's political work with her family's massacre. The woman had worked with her hands all her life, first in her parents' house and then in her husband's house. She had never listened to a radio. She had never learned how to read.

Rita listened and comforted the woman then, but she does not know what became of her in the end. Sometimes at night Rita would fantasize a happy ending to this woman's life story.

Although Rita harboured refugees on several occasions, Altraz found that she was most valuable when she was serving as a distraction for the armed guards, who were everywhere on the streets on Guatemala City. When they were trying to smuggle someone into the city, Rita would often be told to drive or walk by the guards. She had the ability to turn men's heads, and they recognized her wealth in the manicured nails and the designer dresses she wore while she openly flirted with them.

"When they see you, they indulge in the fantasy of having a young woman of the ruling class," Lise would say with a cold edge to her voice. Rita did not like the way Lise said this, but she could not deny it. The words were true enough.

For Rita, "flirting" in this way was an opportunity to rid herself of some of the guilt she was feeling because of her class background. Each time she swayed her hips as she walked by the men with their machine guns that stuck out like enormous obscenities, she knew exactly what she was doing. As she teased them with her white teeth and red mouth, she knew. Their whistles and dirty calls rang in her ears long after she had distracted them from following a car headed for the border, or prevented them from picking a suspicious-looking man out of a line at the bank. Rita knew she was prostituting her class background. Still, she felt a purity about the whole thing. She was doing her part in solidarity with the peoples' movement. She did not feel dirty.

It was not until the following summer that Rita was made to feel dirty.

For a long time Rita didn't tell anyone about what had happened to her that summer at Lake Atitlan in southern Guatemala, and she never told her husband about it. But she believed that the events of that summer had turned her into a liar. And every time she and her husband went to bed together, she felt dishonest.

In telling this story, Rita first told me about her husband. She met him soon after that summer in Lake Atitlan, when her parents sent her away to attend university in Santa Cruz, California. An aunt and uncle lived there, and she stayed with them.

On the day she met Fred, Rita was sitting on a park bench, watching a demonstration expressing solidarity with the people in Central America. A man sat down beside her. He was a young university radical, a little late to be in the thick of the 60s, but not by much. They talked, and as he listened to Rita's Spanish accent and admired her dark complexion, he fancied himself gazing into the face of a real live oppressed person. She was the "real thing." Her class background was buried deep inside her by now. It hid under the white peasant blouse and the clean but faded blue jeans.

Shortly after the day she met and started seeing Fred, she received word that Altraz had been shot. Like magic, she did become a real oppressed person, she told me sarcastically.

Fred was a great help in those awful days after Altraz' death. Altraz had been Rita's favourite brother, almost her idol. Fred helped her shoulder the pain and go on during the following weeks. Years and many arguments later, Rita was still grateful to Fred for his understanding during that time. He would always have a special place in her heart for that reason.

Following Altraz' death, Rita received little comfort from her family. A letter arrived, saying "Stay where you are." She was told, once again, how her parents had sent her to California for her own safety, away from the influence of her foolish brother. It was very dangerous now, the letter continued. The authorities knew of her involvement in her brother's activities. "What pain his stubborn foolishness has visited on your mother," wrote Rita's father. "If anything should harm you, it would kill her."

And from her mother she received this message: "This man you have met, will you be married to him?"

Altraz had been dead a very short while, but the question did not seem out of place to Rita at the time. She believed in the sanctity of marriage. It went along with her Catholic upbringing, and she really needed to believe in something right then. Fred, however, believed in "free love." They compromised. He would marry her. She would follow him to Canada, where he wanted to do postgraduate work in history.

So Rita and Fred were married, in a white wedding ceremony with all the trimmings. It took place at a Roman Catholic Cathedral in Miami, Florida, where Rita's parents had friends, and Rita's family flew in for it. After the ceremony, the celebrations were held at a large club overlooking the Gulf of Mexico. The club belonged to a business associate of her father.

Rita could not read Fred's thoughts. Was he confused? Was his picture of her shattered when he witnessed her family's obvious wealth? Her stomach knotted. How little they actually knew about each other.

For Rita, her family's wedding splash on the Gulf of Mexico was a nice camouflage. Although Fred didn't know about it, she was still working to smuggle people through the States and up to Canada. The death of Altraz had made her even more determined in this. It was her only remaining link with him. Before he was killed she had welcomed any word of him that the refugees could provide. Now, she welcomed a message even from the sour Lise. Although the work with refugees was tiring, and Rita was required to make crucial, quick decisions of a kind seldom made by twenty-year-olds, she had never considered quitting.

Rita and Fred spent their wedding night in a bungalow among the white sands on the gulf. Rita was young and inexperienced, yet she was surprised when she felt pain as her husband penetrated her. There was no blood but she did feel pain. It was anguish for blood that had been forced out of her in her past.

Fred mistook the reason for the pain. Rita saw the pride of ownership in his moonlit eyes. For all his talk about free love, she could see he was proud to think himself the first man to lay on top of her, to be allowed inside. The moon did not allow his thoughts to hide, and Rita knew what he was thinking.

Inside, Rita wept. She could never trust Fred now. Her horrible secret from that summer at Lake Atitlan would be sealed inside her for the rest of her life. It felt like a heavy weight that she would have to lug around with her always. It could never be let out. If she did let it out, Fred, she was sure, would take the side of the enemy. The secret seemed to drop deeper and deeper inside her heart, where it would lodge like a stone.

By September, Rita and Fred were in Toronto. Rita might have forgotten what had happened to her that summer at Lake Atitlan with Altraz and Lise. She might have forgotten, or perhaps remembered it as one does a bad nightmare, for Canada was like a different world from Guatemala or even California. Yet it was here, she knew, that her enemy lived.

At first, she did not comprehend the size of Canada. When she first moved to Toronto she tried to always walk in the shadows of trees. She was positive that the man would find her, defile her again or, perhaps worse, gloat over what he had done to her, over the way he had possessed her without permission, over the fact that she could prove nothing.

So Rita passed her time in Toronto with her eyes down on the ground. Fred began to wonder why he had not noticed a reserved, cold edge to Rita before. She did not mix well with his university friends and made none of her own, although she did well in her studies. She was starting to work on her masters in history. Because she lived in Canada, she took a few courses in Canadian history. Soon she knew more about the country's past than most Canadians did. Still, Fred noticed that Rita had lost a lot of weight, and that her face had became pinched and lined and pale.

When Rita finally let her secret out, it wasn't to Fred. It was to a stranger, a journalist who worked for the leftist press in Toronto. Rita's reputation had preceded her into the progressive community. People got to know through the underground that her brother had been shot because he was connected to solidarity work with the Sandinistas. So the journalist showed up to interview Rita, the surviving sister.

At first Rita did not want to talk with the woman. She was still heavily involved with the underground, bringing her people out of Guatemala and even more out of El Salvador. But the journalist agreed not to use Rita's real name, to camouflage her whereabouts and to talk with her only about the work her brother had been doing when he was murdered. In the article, Rita would be identified only as someone who had worked with him.

The reporter's name was Suzie, and she had an understanding face. By the time she and Rita got together, Rita was very hungry to talk with someone other than her husband or the few university colleagues in whom she was able to confide. Rita and Suzie ended up talking about everything.

Suzie told Rita about her work for the feminist movement. She had come to it gradually after she had moved out of her parent's home in the suburbs and into an apartment in downtown Toronto. Suddenly, out of nowhere, she poured out her story. It was the story of her father, who had raped her continually when she was a little girl and young woman.

At first, Rita did not know where to look. Suzie's pain was almost tangible, something dropping between them as they both stared at it. But Rita pushed down her urge to hug Suzie.

Instead, she wondered aloud, before she could think about stopping herself, why it was wrong when a grown man did this to his daughter but not wrong when a grown man did it to a grown woman.

For example, Rita continued, you have an eighteen-year-old woman, who goes on a holiday with her brother and his lover. It is hot, both politically and literally. The brother thinks it is best to get away from the city for awhile. The three go to Lake Atitlan in southern Guatemala. It is there they meet a gringo from Canada, whose brother owns a bar with a red-and-white Canadian flag tacked onto the wall behind the liquor. There is an American flag on another wall, although the gringo speaks a lot about being in solidarity with the people of Guatemala. The young woman wonders about this but does not dream of questioning her brother's judgement as to whether they should be associating with the Canadian. She thinks her brother must have some secret plans to use the gringo.

The four of them—the brother, his lover, his sister and the gringo—soon start to go everywhere together. They spend afternoons by the water, sitting on towels, swimming, and gazing as if transfixed at the blue volcanic mountains. The gringo takes pictures of the mountains.

In fact, the gringo goes nowhere without his camera. For the young woman, it becomes embarrassing. She laughs, but is serious about wanting him to leave her alone as he insists on taking photo after photo of her. In private, her brother tells her to be nice to the gringo. The revolution needs Canadians, he tells his little sister. And she does admit to herself that she likes the attention she is getting from the gringo. She is scared, but it is more like nervousness than fright. And the man is not unattractive. Still, she is shy of him and his camera, and she is anything but forward with this man. She is unfamiliar with his kind and does not quite know how to act towards him.

In the evenings, they spend hours at the bar. Her brother insists that she drink only Coke. She does not mind. Her brother is showing he cares for her.

As for the gringo, he continues to take pictures of her. Sometimes it is with her brother in the bar. Sometimes she stands alone for the eye of the camera. Sometimes she is with her brother's girlfriend. Sometimes all three of them are together with the gringo, as usual, out of the picture because he is doing the shooting. He is always spying at the young woman through the camera lens. Once when the young woman comments about always being in his pictures, he says he sends the photos back home to make his girlfriend jealous.

"But would she not enjoy a picture of you?" the young woman asks and offers to take it if he shows her how to work the camera. He refuses, absolutely refuses.

Then, one night, the brother is called back to the city unexpectedly. His sister and his lover are told to stay at Lake Atitlan. They are safe there.

But it is on that night, when the brother is not there to insist otherwise, that the gringo puts a little whisky from his shot glass into the young woman's Coke. On that night, and on that night only, the brother's lover excuses herself early. She says she has some letters to write. The next day, the young woman, who shares a room with her brother's lover, sees no letters waiting to be posted. She does not know why the other woman left early. She will never know.

On that night, the gringo says it is okay for her to drink the whisky just that once. But "once" turns into another time and then another. She has never drunk alcohol before, except for the occasional glass of wine at her parents' table. Her head spins. She puts her hands in front of her face when he starts to take pictures, and tells him to stop.

Finally, the gringo's brother, who owns the bar, tells him it is past closing time and he should take the young woman home.

The two weave down the stone street to the water, where they are all staying in a pension with a grass roof. She remembers the stone street because she jabs her sandaled toe against one of the stones.

When they are near the pension, the young woman moves ahead of the gringo, intending to go directly to the room she shares with her brother's lover. But he grabs her arm and says he would like to take a look at her foot, which is bleeding.

"No, no," she says, "I have bandages in my room."

He pulls at her.
He shoves her into his room. He pushes her onto his bed. She
hears her skirt tearing. He rips it off.
He shoves himself into her.
He shoves himself into her.
He shoves himself into her.
Two minutes, maybe less, and it is over.
But it is never over for her.

When Rita came to the end of her story, she realized her voice
had risen. She began to cry, unable to control herself. Suzie
reached over and rocked her gently, as gently as a mother would
a baby. She told Rita the man was wrong for doing what he did
to her, as wrong as Suzie's own father had been.

At Suzie's urging, Rita continued her story. Rita and Lise had
received word from Altraz the following day that they were
needed back in the city. The gringo had said good bye to them
as if nothing had happened. He had even taken a picture of the
two women.

It was April 12. Rita would never forget that date.

Soon afterwards, Rita had been sent to California. Her
parents had discovered that she was involved in Altraz' revolutionary work.

When Rita finished, Suzie encouraged her to become active
in the women's movement in Toronto. In time, through this
involvement, Rita grew stronger and more independent, and she
sought out other Central Americans. She started to make
speeches on behalf of her people.

Fred obtained a teaching position in Winnipeg. They moved,
and things went well for Rita. She had a teaching position. Her
graduate studies were progressing. She met Juanita, and was
grateful to develop such a close friendship with a woman from
her homeland. Inside, she started to heal.

Then, one day when she was cutting across the park to the
apartment building where she and Fred lived, she saw the
gringo. It was him. There could be no mistaking him. And there

was no mistaking her powerlessness to do anything about him. It would be her word, an immigrant's word, against his word.

By day, Rita appeared to be strong as ever. Juanita did not guess that there was anything wrong. No one did. Everyone thought, "What a strong woman Rita is. She is comfortable with power."

At night, when they made love, Rita felt that Fred was forcing his way into the private places of her body.

By springtime, they had separated.

TARA

I get up from my typewriter to find something to eat. As I stuff vegetables and salad dressing into pita bread, I think about Rita. I believe that, during the time I was close to Rita, she continued to struggle with her feelings about the man who had raped her. She kept things under the surface, though, so it was difficult to tell. I was one of a handful of people she had told about the sexual assault and I thought I would quickly lose her friendship if I tried to "work things through" with her. She seldom opened up to others. I did not want her to shut me out.

Sometimes I thought she resented me for knowing her story. I remember one day when Juanita, Rita and I went to a movie together. Afterwards, over coffee, Rita interrupted the conversation. "Oh, Tara with the little green book," she said. "Always going after others to tell their stories and never telling us hers."

As I remember her words, I am eating my salad in front of the English-language evening news. Suddenly my attention is caught by the flickering screen. As expected, the politicians have emerged on the scene of the women's sit-in. They eagerly shout their rhetoric while gesturing for the camera. The women sit and say nothing—except for the woman who reminds me of Rita. Her face is wrinkled with anger and her fist is clenched, though it remains by her side.

My lover Nikos says he knows the women are stronger than the men because they can cry. But Greek men, generally speaking, cry easily—maybe too easily—over things not worth the tears. The women have remained dry-eyed while feeling deep, deep pain. Now that they are crying, I hope the world will take notice. This is something new and different.

The sabre-rattling by the male politicians has clanked on and on, year in and year out. It has become boring and no longer makes "good" world news copy. Not that this is the real point. If the rattling was effective then I would be the first to say, "Rattle on." Nor would it matter how humdrum were the politicians' lines in the old script if something was happening. But nothing is happening. The men have reached a stalemate.

At night when Nikos and I go to the bar, he agrees with me that the women have the right to be angry. Their activity has been the first meaningful action in a long time.

On the late news in the bar, the camera shows women politicians and politicians' wives from Greece stepping off an airplane. They have arrived to show solidarity with their sisters.

I decide I will go, too, and join them on the following day. I can take the bus.

Nikos laughs and pats me on the head. "If you go there they will only ask you why you are not home where you belong with your family in Canada," he says.

"I'm going," I answer, determined.

Next day, I am still in Paphos. I don't know why I haven't gone to Famagusta. I'm restless so I walk up to the market and buy some vegetables and fruit.

On the way back, I climb up onto a knoll covering the top of a cave. I peer out at the aqua-green sea, turning my head west to where, somewhere in the distance, Canada sits.

I hear a rustling of leaves and look down to the east side of the knoll. A woman is plucking mandarin oranges off a tree. From behind, she looks short and stocky like Juanita, with the same wavy black hair pulled back by a flowered kerchief.

I feel the urge to hug Juanita again.

I get up, go back to my flat and back to my typewriter. I can't write for a long time, but when I finally do begin to type, it is about Juanita once again.

JUANITA

$\int$oon after meeting Rodriguez, Juanita was working for the revolution out in the jungle. Rodriguez had decided it was time for them to do so. Work in the jungle was more valuable than what they had been doing in the city.

They were married, although it was nothing more than a formality. Juanita and Rodriguez had been acting like a married couple even before the ceremony. Although Juanita had remained in the house of the American and his wife for awhile longer, she became known as "Rodriguez's woman" and took on a lot of responsibilities. Messages would be given to her to be delivered to Rodriguez, and there was no need for the messenger to instruct or explain things to Juanita. Rodriguez and Juanita had become one.

However, if they were to leave the city together, it was important for them to marry—the Roman Catholic ideas of right and wrong still held great power.

So a priest married Juanita and Rodriguez as they stood in front of him in blue jeans and black leather jackets. A couple, in similar dress, stood by as witnesses. Outside the cathedral, Rodriguez' motorbike was ready to leave the city. Bundles of clothes and a rolled-up tent were tied to its sides.

After the ceremony, they rode quickly towards the jungle, stopping only to relieve themselves on the side of the dirt road. Even though they were moving fast, there was little breeze. As the trees and vines grew thick, the sticky heat seemed to touch their skin.

For three years, Juanita and Rodriguez would live in that dripping heat.

On the day they arrived and set up their tents by the Mayan ruins, they were each given a machine gun. Every morning for the first few days, they would get up with the sunrise and walk further into the jungle. Already Juanita would be thirsty, but she ignored her thirst because there was so much to see and think about. The jungle was a magical, fantastic world protected by vines and ropes of foliage. Behind trees adorned in orchids and bushes growing into more bushes, another world seemed to exist, one protected by the spirits of the Mayans.

The peacocks would dance together each morning in little clearings. Sometimes they would dance over tombstones, swaying, their many-eyed tails open wide as if to better see and honour the new day.

And up ahead of Juanita, the monkeys would swing from vine to tree and tree to vine. Like children eager to get to the picnic site before their parents, they would arrive at the clearing used for target practice long before Juanita and her comrades. They would wait, scratching their fleas.

A man in army fatigues would instruct his followers, who were clad in several different types of uniforms, in the use of machine guns. The gunfire was like the chatter of the enemy, and the monkeys would flee, the snakes would slither away and the birds would sing songs of alarm. The humans would practise killing the enemy.

After they went through this training, Juanita and Rodriguez were given unmatched uniforms, and guns.

Then, they would make their way (together at first, although later they were often apart) through the jungle and to the border, where they would look for bundles. Inside those bundles were more guns. Juanita would pile the guns on her back like a beast of burden, just as her mother had carried vegetables to be sold at market. Her machine gun swung from the strap crossed over one shoulder and between her breasts. Her hands were left free to grab the weapon and use it, if there was a need.

When Juanita made her journey for guns, she would reach a Mayan ruin on the edge of the jungle by evening. At the bottom of the brown stones where her ancestors used to leave their gifts to the gods, Juanita would leave her bundles, her own offerings for social justice in Central America. The bundles would wait there for someone else to take them further south, where yet another person would use them to fight.

One night, Juanita was later than usual. During the day she had experienced difficulty breathing. She had tired early, and was walking slowly to spare the little energy she had left. She didn't dare sit down to rest because danger could come from any direction, particularly if she made herself a stationary target.

Still, her pace had been slower than usual and it was late when she arrived at her destination. The moon was already lighting the ground, providing a backdrop to the flat top of the Mayan pyramid. She hid the guns at the base of the ruin, as usual, and squatted down for a moment to rest her taut muscles. It seemed as if her eyes kept watch, nervously, from every part of her head.

She had raised her gun quickly to shoot when a quetzal fluttered its way through the vines towards her. "Sister," it cried before she could fire. "Sister, sister, sister, sister."

In that moment Juanita knew that the bird was bidding her to follow. It flew up to the room in the flat top of the Mayan monument. So Juanita climbed the stairs carved out of the monument's stone side. It was as if she was walking up through air. When she drew near the top, she could hear someone moaning. It sounded like a wounded person or, possibly, a woman giving birth.

When her eyes grew accustomed to the dark in the room at the top, Juanita saw a naked woman pushing something feathered from between her legs and away from her body. Suddenly, the moon shone on the woman and the gleam of sweat that coated her body gradually turned copper-coloured. Juanita saw the green feathers of a quetzal, tumbling near the black pubic hair of the woman.

This human-born quetzal took flight. Juanita swears she saw it fly to the north. Before she could take even a quick breath, the woman heaved out another bird. It, too, flew north. The woman, her labour finished, curled her legs closed and turned over to her left. She sighed, as if in sexual ecstasy. Yet she was shrivelling up, becoming one with the brown stones under her that had been laid by a slave's hand many centuries before.

Then Juanita saw a dead man in a green uniform, which was tinted yellow in the moonlight. The colours were like pus, pouring out of the eyes and open mouth and dripping out of the sleeve and leg openings in the uniform. It descended upon her, this mucous, turning red like blood. It seemed to crawl from the top of her head where her hair was parted, and creep down over her forehead, nose and mouth, where it broke into two streams. One stream flowed over her body; the other flowed through her mouth. Involuntarily, she swallowed and it lodged, mucous-like, in her lungs.

"I have killed a man," Juanita said out loud, trying to convince herself, trying to make herself feel something. She knew he would have shot her if she had not finished him first. He was the enemy.

Yet she felt nothing. Like an animal, she followed her instincts and ran away. She could not feel her heart beating until she was back in camp and had her arms around Rodriguez.

But in the night, Juanita woke up and clenched her fists, beating at Rodriguez. He woke, surprised, and held her arms behind her back. She spit in his face. In the end she lost because she began to cry. She shouted over and over again that he had led her into committing violence, into murder. "Sí, men are leaders in war," she shouted. "No matter how just the cause, it is too horrible to think about—taking people, guiding people to kill. How can I trust, ever, someone who will do this? You make me stop painting and lead me to this?"

Juanita shouted these things in the middle of the night until her comrades shook their tent. "Quiet," they hissed. "Do you want the enemy to come and finish us all off?"

Juanita finally exhausted herself and slept. In the morning, she woke and put her gun over her shoulder. She knew she would kill again. She had to. She knew this in the end. She would go on killing until there was no more oppression in Central America.

Her heart went back to being empty. (As she talked of this to me, much later, she wondered if this is what people call "thinking like a man.") Two weeks later, she found herself pregnant.

It was her children who brought Juanita to Canada. The eldest, Emmanuel, was a silent baby. His black eyes seemed always to be searching for the enemy. It was as if he had learned from watching his parents that an enemy could be behind any tree, at any time. Juanita's heart broke when she looked into his little face and realized there are no real children in the revolution, just as there are no children in extreme poverty. Emmanuel wore an adult expression on his face.

But, because he was so quiet, Emmanuel did not interfere with his parents' work. And he was no bother to the woman in the nearby village who kept him during the day. At night, he lay between Rodriguez and Juanita in silence. Juanita says he is still silent, even as an adult. She does not understand how he is able to have so many friends, when he is so quiet.

Shortly after Emmanuel's second birthday, Maria came along. From her first breath she wanted the world to know she existed, and she has never allowed the world to forget it since. In the night she would scream at the injustice that made her family's home a tent, that made the air she breathed sticky and thick with humidity, that tried to drain life from her body. She demanded something better.

From the beginning, Juanita felt proud of her daughter. But in the jungle where they were always in danger, Maria's screams terrified everyone. Juanita and Rodriguez were soon confronted by their comrades. They must send their children away, the comrades told them, perhaps to one set of grandparents or the other. The jungle was no place for children.

Juanita met their advice with anger. She knew they were right about the danger that Maria's screams had created for all of them, but she was furious that in a country where it was next to impossible to get reliable birth control, they were saying this place or that place was not a place for children. She wondered how one could stop the children from coming, and she wondered how one could wait for the "right place" in this world.

Rodriguez agreed with the comrades. Did he have nothing to do with these children? Juanita wondered bitterly. Did he think they were fathered by a monkey?

Shortly after Juanita was told to rid the camp of her children, she was walking through the jungle on her way to get weapons, and she began to think about the family's situation. She did not want to miss seeing her children grow up. Her mother, she knew, would be very good with them but her father was growing older, and she feared that he was getting more bad-tempered with each day. She wanted peace for her children. She did not want them reaching adulthood in the middle of the hatred that hung, like the humidity, around them in the jungle. She did not want them to live under the iron rule of her father.

Yet, what else was there? Rodriguez' parents were strangers to Juanita. She had only met them once. However, as Juanita arrived near the spot where the guns were to be stashed on that particular day, she came to the conclusion that this was where they would have to go. Her fear of the known was greater than that of the unknown.

The children would leave and the parents would stay, for the good of the children's future. If she and Rodriguez fought now, Juanita thought, perhaps centuries would pass with no more killing. This was her dream for her children, grandchildren and great-grandchildren.

Then things began to turn out differently. A few days later, a comrade came back from a run to Guatemala City. There were snapshots of Rodriguez being passed around everywhere. The authorities remembered his face from his days as a student radical. They had discovered that he was working as a revolutionary in the guerrilla movement. Word came that they had located his whereabouts.

The comrades decided that Rodriguez and his family must leave. The entire camp was in danger until he did so. The camp would move but, even so, they could not be sure that they were not already being watched. Things had to happen quickly. Rodriguez agreed to go.

So in the middle of the following night they left in a truck, with the moon as their only light. The comrade who drove did not dare turn on the headlights, and they could almost feel the danger. Juanita, Rodriguez, and the children rode in the back of the truck. It grew cold as they left the jungle, on the first leg of a jagged journey that would eventually take them north. Dark green plastic covering the frame on the back of the truck served as an inadequate windbreak. The children slept, though, cuddled close to Juanita's warm body. She had given Maria, the youngest, a sleeping potion so she would not cry out. They were afraid that military guards along the way might drive up in a jeep and block the road in front of them while others waited behind. If that happened, the family would be trapped.

Juanita could not rest. She sat up, stiff with fear. Maybe she had read the message from the quetzal in the wrong way. The bird had come to her on the night of her enemy's death, and had flown north. Maybe this night as they moved north would end in death for the family. Or perhaps death would come the next day or the day after that. Perhaps the quetzal had been warning Juanita against going north, not guiding her there.

Juanita could discern the outline of Rodriguez' back in the blackness. He sat upright near the back of the truck, on guard for his family. Strength seemed to ripple through his arm muscles as he hung on to the tailgate, leaning slightly forward, his head moving from one side to the other while his eyes scoured the countryside. The night went on and on and on.

They were journeying straight north now, and would soon leave their country behind. Rodriguez told Juanita to wake the children, to say goodbye. He told them to remember where they had come from, and to remember their beautiful country with pride. Much later when she told me of this journey, Juanita thought that maybe the children had been too sleepy to hear him properly; she doubted that they would want to return now, even if it were possible.

The small family arrived at the border of Mexico before morning. They got out of the truck and the comrade quickly turned the grey truck around and was gone. No one waved. They were comrades, not friends.

The family crawled across the border, at a place where the guard was known to be drunk and sleeping. Maria was rolled up in a blanket and tied to Juanita's back. The sleeping potion still protected them from her cries.

On the other side, where someone was supposed to meet them, there was no one. They began walking. To stay in one place would be committing suicide. They had food and water enough for one day, and the clothes on their backs. This was as close to having nothing as Juanita had ever been or felt. Yet, she said much later, she felt a strange freedom, as if she was standing on the edge of a cliff and looking down into a green valley.

Then a wave crashed against her body and the fear returned. By noon, when the sun was baking their skins and replacing moisture with dust, a truck stopped for them. Inside was a Mexican. He greeted them and asked where they had come from. Rodriguez gave the name of a small village they had passed an hour earlier. "Funny," the Mexican responded, "I live there and I don't know you."

"We live in the hills," Rodriguez answered, too quickly.

The Mexican knitted his eyebrows together for a moment and then he laughed. He took off his straw hat, and shifted it to the back of his head in order to get a better look at the Guatemalans. "Maybe it is in the hills very close to the border, sí?" he asked. "I have been up there this morning to look for a man, his woman and two children."

They all laughed then, in relief. The Mexican told them to get in and he would drive them to the Gulf, to the home of his brother-in-law, who fished there.

In the back of the truck, the Guatemalans hid among bananas. Some of the yellow pieces of fruit had broken open. Juanita and Rodriguez fed them to the children. Then, beneath the shade of the banana leaves, which filtered the sun onto their skin like embroidery, the family took an afternoon siesta.

It was dark but still warm by the time they felt cool, offshore breezes. The truck stopped and the driver came around to the back to tell them to wait inside for awhile. They could hear voices arguing. Finally, a new voice—that of the brother-in-law—agreed to take them across the Gulf in the early morning when he set out to fish. He could not afford to make a special trip. And they would sleep by the water for the night. His wife could make no room for them in the house.

So the family crawled out of the truck, and onto the white sand dunes. The truck driver gave Rodriguez some American money—enough to get the family to a sympathizer's house in Miami when they reached the other side. Rodriguez tied the bills in a dotted handkerchief and knotted it to his belt. Their Mexican friend left.

They sat in silence.

In the darkness, Juanita thought of death. She was not prepared to die, but she was not frightened of it either. It was the torture they would be sure to put her through first that frightened her. She thought of childbirth and how, if you've never experienced it, you think you will never make it through.

But maybe pain or death was not the worst of it. Juanita felt in her guts that they could take her soul. They could finish her off totally. It was beyond comprehension and imagination—being made into nothing.

Then Juanita's mind grew very, very tired. She curled her body around her daughter. She felt the cool of the white sand against her cheek. Maybe it was as cool as snow, Juanita thought, as she realized fully for the first time that they were headed for Canada. Snow fell like little sprinkles of water on her face, on her hands, on her arms, on her bare legs under her dress up to her underpants. It swept over her.

Juanita woke. Waves were lapping her body. She shook Rodriguez, so that he and the boy would not get wet. "It will be good to us ... Canada," she told her husband, and kissed him.

After that, they were silent. To the east, the sky was already streaked with orange. To the north, everything was still dark. Juanita thought of snow and how, in her dreams, it had taken her thirst away.

Soon the fisherman came, and motioned for them to follow him to his boat. The children and Juanita climbed into the boat, and Rodriguez and the fisherman pushed it into the clear, green water. It was as if they were shattering the water's flat glass surface. Juanita ran her hand through the water. It was still very cold.

When they were all in the boat, the man handed Rodriguez a small plastic bag. It was filled with tacos and beans. Juanita ate one hungrily as she nursed Maria, while Rodriguez saw that some food got into Emmanuel's belly. The little boy wanted only to point his finger out toward the north, and smile in delight at the cool breeze which rose off the gulf.

Somewhere halfway between the land now to their south and that ahead of them to the north, the man stopped the boat and, with Rodriguez' help, placed his nets in the water. Then on they went to the far side.

Before they reached Stateside, the boat halted again. The man asked if they could swim. Yes, they could. "Good," the man replied. He dared not go any closer to the white beach on the north side. The Miami coast guard might be out. One had to be careful. But first, he insisted on drinking to their good luck. He pulled out a half-full bottle of Tequila and took a large gulp before passing it to Rodriguez.

Rodriguez took a gulp, grimaced and threw himself into the sea like a man on fire. Then he turned to take Emmanuel. He towed his little boy towards the far beach. Juanita followed with Maria strapped on her back.

Fortunately, the sea was calm. As they got out of the water, they could hear the sound of the boat turning south. Instinct made Juanita and Rodriguez turn and wave good-bye, although the Mexican did not look back.

Then, summoning all their courage, Juanita and Rodriguez stripped off their own clothes and their children's clothes and hung them on bushes to dry. Much later, in Canada, Rodriguez would joke about walking into North America with not even the clothes on their backs.

In an hour or so, their things were dry. They dressed, and walked up and over the dunes until they came to the highway. They turned in the direction they knew must be east and headed towards Miami. If they could make it there, everything would be alright. The friend of their people would surely take care of them, they believed, although they dared not trust completely in a man they had not yet met. In the meantime, they had to take chances. The children could not walk very far, and carrying them was too tiring. They came to a sign that read "Miami 52." Rodriguez began to wave at cars.

For a long time, no car would stop. Finally, two or three hours later, a car did stop. It was a police car. They turned to run into the bushes but the voice that reached their ears spoke in Spanish, in the Mexican dialect. The police officer promised not to harm them. They had to believe him—where could they run to?

The officer invited them into his car. Juanita sat in the back seat with her hand on the door handle. She was sure Rodriguez was doing the same in the front seat. Each parent held a child. The officer asked if they knew they were not supposed to be hitch-hiking. Rodriguez said, no, they were newcomers. The officer held up his hand. He would prefer not to know the details of where they were from, he said. But where were they going? Rodriguez told him they were heading to Miami.

Slowly, the police officer pulled a toothpick out of his shirt pocket. He chewed it and looked straight ahead at the white lines on the highway. He would drive them to the outskirts of the city, he said. "But, for God's sake," he warned, "remember to remain in the bush until night, once I drop you off." He wondered why they had not been warned against travelling out in the open in the daylight.

While they drove along, the police officer told them about an orange grove up ahead. It would be a good place to sleep through the day. He offered them his lunch, saying his wife fed him much too well anyway. Finally, they reached the grove. "Adios," said the officer. The ride had seemed to take forever, but the good-bye was mercifully quick.

For the rest of the day, the family crouched like animals under a tree. The tree had branches heavy with oranges ripe for the picking, ready to wet sandpaper-dry mouths. But each time a leaf rustled, Rodriguez and Juanita would shift towards the children, ready to grab them and run.

By mid-afternoon the heat, even under the tree, was pressing into them, oppressing them. They slept, while the sweat poured out of them. Juanita kept her hand over Maria's mouth, even in her sleep, in case the baby should wake and cry out.

Juanita herself felt like crying. Only two days ago she had been in her homeland. Now she was half a world away from where she belonged. Things were moving so fast. She slept fitfully, and each time she woke she noticed Rodriguez fumbling with the money in the kerchief. He sorted through it again and again, as if searching for some clue on its ugly green paper that would tell him how much to use when the time came to purchase something. This man, with his confidence fluttering, seemed strange to Juanita.

Finally, the darkness hid them. They stuffed some oranges into the now-empty lunch bag given to them by the police officer. Then they walked through damp, long grass growing between the trees and down into the ditch along the highway. They kept to the low ground, although they had been taught never to travel where the enemy could spot them from higher ground. But Rodriguez and Juanita had agreed that they could not walk in the path of the blinding car headlights, and expose themselves to even greater harm. Who knew what was behind those lights?

After awhile they had to move onto the sidewalk, where it met and replaced the ditch. It wound along two lanes of highway and then four, as they got closer and closer to the flashing lights of the city.

Sweat poured out of Juanita, and she began counting in her head, holding onto each number like it was an old friend until the next one came to mind. It took a lot of energy to remember each number when she felt so much fear and confusion. She dared not stop counting, for if she did, she was certain she would turn and run—and there was nowhere for her to go, nothing but a dead end. Still, the noise of traffic tried to grab the numbers away from her. She held Maria tighter and tighter until her daughter screamed in discomfort.

Maria's noisy protest reminded Juanita that she was a

mother. Her arms relaxed. From somewhere deep inside her, she imagined a cool breeze brushing over her skin. Then she looked at Rodriguez. His smile visited her as a friend. It had been a long time since she had thought about her love for him.

They came at last to a motel with a Spanish name. Juanita stopped with the children as Rodriguez followed the driveway. She knew what to do without the need for conversation. In the distance, she saw Rodriguez approaching a man in a rocking chair on the porch outside the motel office.

They quickly discovered that it was alright to stay there. The man spoke Spanish, and perhaps did not even overcharge them. It was hard to say, for Rodriguez opened his fistful of American dollars to this stranger and asked him to pick out what was his.

The children and Juanita waited in their room as Rodriguez, with the motel-owner's help, placed a phone call to the man in Miami who was to help them go north to Canada. The room was small and dusty, but it was cool, and out of the tap in the rusty sink came water. It tasted strong, like medicine, from the chlorine. Still Juanita and the children drank many glasses, moistening their throats as if an artesian well had suddenly sprung up out of desert sand.

Soon Rodriguez returned to tell Juanita that their comrade would come pick them up and take them to his place after midnight. By then his neighbours would be asleep.

For a few hours, the Guatemalans slept. When the knock came on the door, Juanita woke in terror. She thought it was them—the enemy—coming to take the family. But the man at the door was small and quite inconspicuous in a dark business suit with a white handkerchief folded in the breast pocket. His black hair was neatly cropped and he had a clipped mustache. Could this be their comrade, or was he going to turn them over to the authorities?

As if he could read Juanita's mind, the man said, "The clothes of the revolutionary come in many styles." In the dim light, Juanita saw his mouth flash open into a white smile.

Later, they discovered he disguised himself not only with his dress but also with the flower shop he and his wife owned. It was an effective disguise, and he had helped many refugees get to Canada. His secret was not in hiding himself, but in letting people think he was someone he really was not.

The man took Juanita and her family to his home in his small but spotlessly clean car. It was still very dark when they got there and he took them downstairs to the recreation room. He pulled a bed out of the couch and handed Juanita some blankets. In four hours it would be time for his wife to rise for the day. He promised she would prepare a big breakfast for them at that time. Now, he suggested, it would be best for all of them to get some sleep.

In the morning, the señora cooked a huge breakfast for the family, and served it on white plates. There were eggs and tacos and even pancakes, and jugs of freshly-squeezed orange juice. Juanita ate as slowly as she could, not wanting to spill food on the snow-white tablecloth. She watched the children closely. Coming as they did from life in a tent, this was the first time they had eaten at a table.

As the plates emptied, the señora brought more and more food to fill them. When she wasn't doing that, she stood by the door to the kitchen and drank strong coffee.

Finally, the man moved back from his plate, wiped his lips and belched. He talked of how he and his wife had not been blessed with children, and he smiled at Juanita's bambinos. He told his wife to ask around at the shop. She nodded and, Juanita thought, looked a bit sad. But Juanita was too polite to ask what they meant.

"Now," the man said, "you, Rodriguez, will come with me. I think we will find a way for you to move north at the harbour. My wife will tend to the flower shop today. And you," he pointed at Juanita, "will stay in the basement all the day with the children. This, above all, is very important. You hear a knock at the door, you don't answer it, sí?"

The woman led Juanita and the children back downstairs and the little ones were put back to sleep. Juanita was handed towels and one of the señora's dresses, and shown to the shower stall in the basement.

Under the shower, as the cool water sprayed over her body, Juanita dreamed of Lake Atitlan and its mountain springs. She promised herself that she would keep those memories. From that day on, she promised, if someone pitied her for the loss of her homeland, she would go over those memories of Lake Atitlan in her mind.

Once out of the shower, Juanita was uneasy. It was very silent and cool in the dim basement. After putting on the dress left for her by her hostess, she went over to the small, high window and pulled the curtain aside so that a crack of the outside world was visible.

It looked sunny and hot outside, like the day before. Some of the houses, she noticed, had Spanish-style roofs and white, stuccoed sides like those belonging to the rich in Guatemala City. But there was no one out on the streets. This was so different from home, where everyone would be out working on the streets and enjoying the sunny morning. Here, things seemed deserted and the air was heavy with silence. She turned from the window and wept into her hands. At least sounds could still come out of her own throat, she thought.

Perhaps she cried herself out in the morning, for she had no tears in the evening when bad news was delivered to her. The men had finally returned. By the time they got back, Juanita had become completely bored with looking at hairstyles in the glossy magazines she had pulled from the rack under the coffee table. She greeted the men gladly, but their smiles in return were uneasy.

First, they had news about their success in discovering a way for Juanita to enter Canada. She immediately wondered why they spoke of her alone, but she let them go on. Down at the harbour, a friend of a friend knew a couple who were doctors, and who were sympathetic to the Left in their politics. In response to Juanita's question, the man explained further. They were rich people, very wealthy in fact, but were willing to help the poor and had open minds about those on the Left. These particular people just happened to live in the city of Winnipeg, the same city where Rodriguez' cousin lived. They spent their winters in Miami and returned north, in the motor home, for the summer. They had agreed to take Juanita back to Winnipeg as their domestic servant.

Rodriguez would follow, the man continued. It was best, according to Canadian policy at that time, for him to go to the border by bus. His cousin could meet him at the border and, as a guest of his cousin, he could apply for a work visa and landed immigrant status from within the country. If the whole family tried to get in together as refugees they would have difficulties, for Canada was taking in more people who were fleeing from communist regimes than it was taking people escaping military dictatorships.

"So what of my babies?" Juanita wanted to know. She began to shiver in that cool, damp basement. They would have to stay in Miami, she was told, until she and her husband had saved the money for them to follow. With their parents already working in Canada, the officials would not be so cruel as to turn them away, providing they could prove that there was enough money to support them.

Rodriguez would not look into Juanita's eyes. The reflection in his black eyes of a bold soul, and a leader from their student days, was gone. They were not in control of their lives anymore. Juanita winced as a certain thought went through her mind: she had left her homeland in order to remain with her children and now she would have to go on without them. Rodriguez, she knew, was thinking the same thing, but they did not exchange their thoughts aloud. They were foreigners now, refugees. Their lives were in other peoples' hands. Whether or not those people were good to them, they would be grateful.

The next piece of news from the men was ominous. The comrade had noticed a car following them earlier in the day. It was best for all concerned that Juanita and Rodriguez move on quickly.

The señora had brought a big Mexican woman home with her that evening. This was the woman who would care for Juanita's children. She had raised six children of her own, and all of them had moved away to different parts of the country. This was the

American way, the Mexican woman said. If she was lucky she got the grandchildren during school vacations.

With her rough red hands, she patted the heads of Juanita's children. For the boy, she had brought a Mexican puppet with a straw hat, thick black eyebrows and mustaches, a bright purple vest and pistols stuck to his brown sleeves; and for Maria she had brought a soft teddy bear. In her heart, Juanita knew her children would be well looked after.

And they were. But rarely did a minute pass during the coming months of separation when Juanita did not yearn to call them by their pet names and hear and see and feel them responding. Over those months she sometimes imagined that the smell of their freshly washed heads after she had bathed them was in her nostrils.

Next, Rodriguez phoned his cousin. Rodriguez looked like he didn't quite believe what was happening, but nonetheless arrangements were quickly made for his departure. Late that night, a bus would be leaving for Chicago and, from there, he would catch another to Minneapolis and on to the border of Canada. His cousin would be there to greet him and assure the authorities that Rodriguez was his guest, to feed and house for three months.

Meanwhile, Juanita would probably already be across the border with her ... who were they? she asked herself ... her masters. Juanita was soon to find that these people insisted upon being called her employers, not her masters.

As Rodriguez was making his phone call and they discussed Juanita's future, she was watching their host. His movements were jerky. He was impatient and nervous, she realized. He was hurrying things along. The children must go, he told the Mexican woman, and she took them quickly. There was no way to keep them, Juanita realized, and she did not have the words to bid them good-bye.

Soon the comrade gave them bus directions, and Rodriguez and Juanita were quickly shown out the door. They were once again strangers in a strange world.

Outside it was still hot. They walked down the street, as

people watched them from windows. One could tell there were people around by the banging of a door or the smell of smoke from a barbecue. Still, they were not out on the sidewalks laughing with their neighbours, like the people in Juanita's village. At most, some stared at the Guatemalans from their fenced-in backyards, their eyes narrow slits.

On the corner where they had been instructed to wait for the bus, Juanita and Rodriguez stood for a long time. Juanita looked down at her borrowed dress. When she had put it on, it felt soft and smelled of laundry detergent—the kind used in an automatic washing machine. Its yellow and orange flowers, printed on brown cloth, had looked pretty. Now she realized that the dress was much too long and that her brown sandals were falling apart, too. She was poor, she felt, like a woman with nothing beautiful is poor.

Finally, the bus came and they got on. Juanita walked with her head down, avoiding the stares of the passengers. Behind her, she heard the clang of the silver money as Rodriguez placed it in the metal fare box. Newspapers rustled as more eyes gawked at them.

They sat at the back of the bus. Juanita's bare legs stuck to the seat, which had been left sticky by the sweat from a hot day's passengers. After a long while, they noticed a hotel. The comrade had advised them to get off the bus once they had passed this landmark, and Rodriguez' eyes had been glued to the streets, watching for it. He forgot himself in his anxiety to get off at the right stop, and yelled at the driver to stop.

The driver sped up at the sound of Rodriguez' voice. Juanita and Rodriguez ran up to the front. The driver barked at them to use the back door if they wanted to get off. "Sí," Rodriguez said hastily and then realized his error. "Yes, yes," he corrected himself in answer to the driver's scowl, and out the back they went. On the sidewalk, they began the kilometre-long walk back to where they had wanted to get off in the first place.

Rodriguez left Juanita quickly. The last couple of days had turned him into a stranger. As he walked back to the bus stop,

Juanita noticed how bent his shoulders were. She still wanted to bolt and run, but not after him.

That night, Juanita slept in the wealthy Canadians' motor home. She dreamed of watching the Marlon Brando movie with Rodriguez. In her dream, she could see they were going to sit through to its ending. She forced herself awake. She was too scared to go on watching.

When the Canadians reached the border, the border guards were told that Juanita was a domestic servant. The guards talked with Juanita's wealthy employers and did not ask her direct questions. They did not even ask her name.

Things slowed down and were, in some ways, very ordinary for Juanita during her first while in Canada. Her life took on a routine, although her surroundings and the customs of the country were quite new.

The doctors were good to Juanita, she told me. The room above the garage where she stayed was larger than the house in which she had grown up. It had a kitchen and a living space with a comfortable couch and a television. There was a nice sea-blue rug on the floor. In the bathroom, there was a shower and a flush toilet. The bedroom had a soft queen-sized bed with a yellow electric blanket under the floral-pattern comforter.

In the evening, after her work was finished in the main house, Juanita would take a shower. When she stepped out of it, she would often glance at the glass door of the shower, where her reflection looked back at her from behind a design of two white swans taking off into flight.

Then she would put on her navy flannel pyjamas (given to her by her employers) and turn on the television. She would turn it up loud to drown out the silence while she fixed her evening meal. But the voices never talked away her loneliness. They spoke foreign words, not the language she longed to hear, although they did help improve her English.

Soon she would go to sleep. Sleep served to block her fears about Rodriguez and the well-being of her children. And morning came early. Each work day would begin in the same way. She would cross through the garden, pass the marble statue of a Greek goddess, and go through the back entrance into the kitchen.

Once inside, she would see the other domestic worker, Jamael, a black woman from the Caribbean. The doctors had told Juanita that Jamael spoke Spanish, but Jamael made no attempt to speak in Spanish to the Guatemalan. "Hmpf," Jamael would say, enunciating in English. "Mrs. says you have children in Florida. You think you'll ever see them again? Hah, six years ago I come to dis place. I think in a year I bring my children here. They still not here, Missy. I see them only on holidays on two occasions," Jamael would wave two fingers in the air, "when I return to Bahamas."

For the longest time, Jamael had no friendly words for Juanita. She seemed to delight in reminding her co-worker of how remote was the possibility of a reunion with her family. And it was true that even Rodriguez had not arrived as he had promised. He wrote to Juanita to say he was picking fruit for the summer on his way through the States and would arrive in the fall. It was a means for him to earn some money so that the children could be back with their parents as soon as possible. Juanita read the letter over and over again. The pen with which Rodriguez had written the letter must have been scratchy and running out of ink, and this made the message seem very unclear. There was nothing for Juanita to do but wait. In the meantime, she would try to wash the redness and puffiness out of her eyes each morning, so that Jamael would not realize she had been crying in the middle of the night.

Jamael prepared the food and Juanita served at the table. After breakfast, they would scrape the plates and place them in the dishwasher. Then the two women would get out the cleaning trolley, similar to the ones used in hotels. The chemicals often started Juanita sneezing. It was making her sick, using these products to kill bacteria and make everything white, white, white.

The two women would climb in the elevator to the main part

of the house, and clean bathrooms with tubs the size of swimming pools. Then they would move back down to the ground floor, where they would vacuum the cream-coloured carpet. Juanita would feel like she was wading through that carpet, it was so deep. Once a week it had to be shampooed. When the furniture on the ground floor had been dusted, Juanita would go back up to the bedrooms while Jamael returned to the kitchen to start preparing lunch. It was Juanita's job to make the beds and straighten things in the upstairs rooms.

The doctors had a son, and when Juanita reached his room, her stomach would tighten. This young man was in his twenties, and he looked like a "hippie" to Juanita. A large black-iron peace symbol hung on his door.

Each day the same thing would happen between Juanita and the son, just as the cleaning seldom differed from one day to the next. Juanita would give his closed door a tap. He would shout through the door that whoever was out there should fuck off, but Juanita did not dare leave. One time she had gone away, only to witness the son complain to his parents at the evening meal that his room had not been cleaned. The doctors had looked at Juanita coldly. If they had one weakness it was their son. On the following day, Juanita knocked and knocked again, despite the obscenities hurled at her through the closed door. She was in Canada because of the goodwill of her employers. She could not afford to be thought of as a lazy worker.

So, each day Juanita would knock a second time and each day she would be greeted with another string of curses before the son walked over to the door and pulled it open. He would stand there nude, and then, with the door wide open and Juanita's eyes cast down to the carpeted floor, he would climb into patched jeans. Next, he would pull on his army shirt and a string of beads.

Juanita would begin making the bed. Its satin sheets were cool to the touch. But they stank of unwashed socks and were flecked with dirty blonde hair from the son's greasy head. Behind her, on the other side of the room, he would crank up heavy metal music on the stereo and flop down onto the floor, where he would prop pillows behind his head and light up a marijuana joint. All the while, his eyes would comb the backside of the maid.

Juanita would move over to the French windows, which led out onto a balcony, to shake out pillows and get some air circulating into the room. Her head was already pounding.

Back inside the room, as she went about tidying, the son would invariably move up behind her and dig his nails into her buttocks. It was very painful, and extremely humiliating.

Towards the end of her time at the doctors' place, Juanita began to get physically sick upon leaving the son's room. She would vomit into the toilet in the small bathroom at the corner of the hall.

Rodriguez finally arrived in the fall. He stayed at his cousin's place. Juanita was then given one day a week to be with her husband. They would come together at the cousin's rented house, downtown on Spence Street. She would talk to Rodriguez about the problems she was having in her employment and he promised they would soon rent a room of their own and things would be better.

Juanita would return to work after her Sunday off feeling optimistic. She resolved to save her money towards renting a room of their own, which they needed before they could think of bringing their children to be with them. Rodriguez, she knew, had earned only enough to continue his travel to Canada. The wages for the kind of work he had been doing were small, and the bosses could spot illegal aliens as soon as they came looking for work. Now, in Canada, it was taking a long time for Rodriguez to obtain a work visa. He could only take under-the-table jobs washing dishes and loading trucks, whenever his cousin heard of someone who needed help. And the wages for these tasks were small.

As time went on, Juanita began to realize that Rodriguez was only pretending that he was saving money. She was doing all the saving. She did not make much, but it was still more than Rodriguez, and Rodriguez insisted on paying his cousin rent, while Juanita had her place above the garage for nothing.

Finally, the day came when Juanita had enough money for a

deposit and three months rent on a room in the downtown area. She handed it to Rodriguez in his cousin's livingroom, where they slept on a pull-out couch. His ego from the old days got the better of him, and his anger spilled out as he tossed the money onto the floor.

But the next morning, before the cousin and his family rose for the day, Rodriguez stooped down to the floor and picked it all up. He stuffed it into his wallet while Juanita put on her clothes. He handed over the money for the room to the rental agency later that week.

Things were better then. In the night, Juanita would leave the doctors' mansion and return to the room by nine o'clock. There, she would find Rodriguez hunched over a wood carving, like the old men back home. To fill in the long hours of each day when his spirits fell lower and lower, he had taken to whittling.

But things were better during the nights Rodriguez and Juanita spent together. Each evening, she would sit with him and tell stories about her days, and by morning Juanita would leave for work knowing she had helped raise her husband's spirit.

They were just little things that Juanita related to Rodriguez. About going to Safeway, for instance, which was so different from shopping in the open markets back home where only tourists too naive or shy to barter would pay the price asked. Juanita would show Rodriguez a shiny, waxed green pepper that looked like the plastic vegetables and fruits with which the Americans and wealthy Guatemalans decorated their dining-room tables back in Guatemala City. Then she would cut into the vegetable and eat a piece of it, to prove to Rodriguez that it was real food. She told, too, of standing in long lines and waiting for one's turn to pay the high prices one had no choice but to pay. All this was new and strange.

Rodriguez would listen, his head on Juanita's lap, as she told him these things. "How clean and tidy the buses are here," she would say, "and everyone faced forward with their heads not daring to look left or right." Rodriguez would laugh and forget his futile hunt for work. They never tired of discussing the differences between Canadian lifestyles and those they had known back home in Latin America. They grew into friends. It was only in Canada, without his comrades, that Rodriguez turned to Juanita for friendship.

Juanita was happy. She started to save money for the bus fares that would bring her children up to Canada. It was difficult to put aside any money at all after the rent was paid, but their little apartment ensured that there was a place for her children to stay. Juanita no longer had any doubt that the family would be reunited.

At work, Jamael was still giving Juanita trouble, but that suddenly changed, too, when the doctors announced that they had found Juanita a job with a friend who lived across the park from them. He was a garment-factory owner and Juanita could work for him as a sewing-machine operator. The pay would be somewhat better than what the doctors could afford to pay her and really, they told Juanita, they could not afford to have two servants. Things were getting worse economically, and there would be an opening for Juanita at the factory in a month.

That was a day of surprises for Juanita. She was surprised at her employers' statement about hard economic times. She marvelled about this as she waded through the thick cream-coloured carpet outside the study where they had told her of the new job. It was impossible for her to imagine what good economic times must be for the rich in this country.

The second surprise came from Jamael. When Juanita left for home that evening, Jamael gave her a bag of leftovers from supper. Juanita did not know what to make of this and hesitated before accepting it. What if this was a trick and Jamael went to the doctors with a story that the woman from Guatemala was stealing? "Go on now and take it," Jamael said with a smile on her face. "Mrs. don't like food going to waste and the doctor don't like leftovers more than once a week." (Jamael refused to acknowledge that the woman was a doctor, too).

On the bus going home, Juanita wondered about the sudden change in Jamael. Somewhere around the point where the bus crossed the bridge and passed the hospital, it dawned on her. Jamael had been worried that Juanita might take her job away.

This was a strange, strange country, Juanita thought. There was so much wealth yet people were scared for their jobs.

Each night for the entire month that followed, Jamael gave Juanita a bag of leftovers. Juanita was glad to take it, because it meant more of her money could go into the savings that would bring the children to Canada, and she did not have to spend her time cooking when she got home.

Maybe, Juanita thought, after she had brought her own children to Canada she could provide Jamael with some money to help bring Jamael's children to Canada. Yes, she could leave it in an envelope addressed to Jamael, with no return address. It would be a secret gift to a woman who could not help but be bitter with her children so far away for six years. The idea gave Juanita a lot of pleasure.

With the new job came more good news. Rodriguez had finally received his work visa and he, too, got a job. In his case, it was at the aircraft factory. Fourteen months after Juanita had arrived in Canada, the children joined her and Rodriguez, and another was already beginning to grow in Juanita's belly.

Jamael was not to be so fortunate.

Juanita explained what happened to Jamael by first telling me about Rodriguez' English lessons, which he took at a nearby high school two evenings a week. Each afternoon, on her way home from work, Juanita would get off the bus one stop early and pick up the daily newspaper for Rodriguez. If he was not too tired, he would show her the spelling of English words and explain their meaning so that she, too, could expand her knowledge of the language. Often they would read aloud the words they didn't understand and Rodriguez would later ask his instructor for the meanings of the words.

It became a bit of a game. Some evenings, after picking up the children at the daycare on Broadway, Juanita would get a chance to sit down with the newspaper for a few minutes before Rodriguez got home. She would put her feet up on the old coffee table near the couch and look at all the pictures, trying to decipher the captions under them.

One day, this is what she was doing when she stopped in

disbelief. A black woman had been killed while pushing a shopping cart across the street. In the background of the photograph there was a Safeway. Juanita knew it had to be the one near the doctors' home. The photograph showed everything. The scarf next to the body had large daffodils, like the one Jamael always wore. The body was stout, like Jamael's. And there was Jamael's huge leather purse, squashed in on top of the boxes of cat food that stuck out of the grocery bags. That purse seemed to be waiting for the woman to get up and brush off her coat. But Jamael was never going to get up again. Rodriguez read the caption when he arrived home. It was Jamael. She had died instantly.

The funeral was on a Friday. On the Saturday, Juanita went to The Bay, where she bought paints and a cheap, but presentable, canvas. Jamael's face, and the unknown faces of Jamael's children, would not leave Juanita's mind. Those poor children, she thought, to grow up with no mother at all, not even one several countries away.

Juanita began to paint the face on that Saturday night as soon as her own children were put to bed. Rodriguez watched her uneasily, but silently, as she picked up the brush to paint once more. He could not deny her this work in memory of Jamael. In any case, even if he had tried to stop her, Juanita would have gone on.

At first Juanita found it was difficult to paint. It had been years since she had last held a brush. The painting took a long time to finish and the work was painstakingly slow. Juanita's hands moved like they had when she was learning to paint with the American artist. But somewhere deep inside of her, she wanted this painting to last.

Then she started to think that if she took her time to finish the portrait, she might have found a way to persuade Rodriguez that she should do another painting and another and another. There were so many things in this new land to put down on canvas. Juanita's mind rushed and somersaulted with thoughts of them all.

When Juanita could do no more with her depiction of Jamael,

she visited the doctors and got the address in the Bahamas where Jamael's children stayed. The painting was packaged up and sent south, with a letter from Juanita about her experience working with their mother. She wrote that Jamael had been a good woman, and she hoped the painting would be accepted by them in remembrance of Jamael.

Months later, with a new baby at her breast, Juanita opened a letter from Jamael's sister, who wrote that words could not express their gratitude for the picture.

The urge to paint swelled up in Juanita. She was on maternity leave with her new baby. The baby, as luck would have it, enjoyed sleep, lots of it. So after the baby was put down for the afternoon, Juanita would open the windows to let the paint fumes drift out into the summer air where the baby and Rodriguez, who arrived home around four, would not smell them.

Juanita made a painting of that baby in the little, brown apartment. Then she felt compelled to paint the other children: Maria playing at the daycare centre; Emmanuel making a snow-man beside the sidewalk to the apartment building. This was her family in Canada. This was their environment, their back-ground, now.

After her maternity leave was over, Juanita went back to working outside the home. Still, she thought, she could paint—maybe in the late evening when the others were in bed. Surely she could persuade Rodriguez to allow her this much.

In the end, Juanita never bothered asking Rodriguez. Very soon after giving birth, she found herself pregnant again. Preg-nancy was something she seemed to be always blessed and always cursed with. She was fed up, she told the doctor after this new baby had arrived. "Look," she said, "there is good birth control in this country, no?"

"Well," the doctor said, "I wouldn't say 'good,' but yes, there is quite effective birth control." So Juanita went home and told Rodriguez that the doctor had said she was finished with having babies. She did not say that the birth control pill would prevent the pregnancy.

But it was too late already. Where was the time to paint, with her work (now in the aircraft factory with Rodriguez) and the children very small and getting into everything and wanting to know everything? Juanita could not keep her mind clear. When she did paint, the work showed her confusion and not much of anything else. There was no time to untangle for the canvas the thoughts in her mind, the feelings in her heart. And, besides, Rodriguez was still breathing down her neck. This struggle over her right to paint and to express herself with her art was one of their few conflicts.

So Juanita was stuck with a desire she could not satisfy. Her desire was heightened even more when she became known as a midwife in the Latin American community and began to assist at births once more. She delighted in doing this work, but felt low and sad after each delivery. There was a void she knew she would never fill unless she could commemorate those new lives. She wanted to document the wonder of women's bodies as they released so much beauty.

Soon women who had lived in Canada all their lives and members from other immigrant communities were asking for Juanita's skills as a midwife. When she rested after the babies had been born, Juanita's eyes took in the dressers and clothes in the bedrooms, the wall hangings, the talismans that surrounded the women as they gave birth. And she noted the waves of their hair, the twist of their bodies. The women were not so different from each other, but their style of clothes and the way they wore their hair or painted their faces was. Their surroundings were very new to Juanita—as new as each baby. Juanita's mind cleared when she soaked up these things, but still there was no time to paint.

Then, one day, a tall, beautiful woman with sunglasses covering her dark eyes visited the factory where Juanita worked. This woman was dressed in an immaculate dark suit—a blazer and a skirt with black stockings and leather high-heeled shoes. She was doing research, Juanita overheard the woman tell the boss, on the role of women in the aircraft factory industry since World War II. The woman spoke English with a Spanish accent.

"Hey, take off your glasses and see what is really going on here," Juanita shouted in Spanish, over the din on the floor. "Research? I will tell you where the women are here: in the lowest paying jobs, along with the immigrant men—the immigrant men and refugees." The factory had its sweatshop flavour and Juanita had eyes and ears. Her paycheque never seemed to compensate for her aching back after bending over conveyor belts all week.

"You will tell me," the tall woman said, in Spanish. Her name was Rita and that was the first day of a close friendship between the two women. Rita was very free and feminist, Juanita thought. For her part, Rita urged Juanita to get involved in the feminist movement. "Look," she would say, "your husband is now spending a lot of time in that political theatre group. Do you not have the right to go out your door sometimes after dark or on a Sunday afternoon?"

Juanita knew Rita spoke the truth. Rodriguez had found comrades in their new country, while she found it difficult to get away from the house.

Rodriguez and Rita did not like each other. This was clear upon their first meeting. On her many visits to their home, Rita never attempted to hide her dislike for Rodriguez. She always looked him straight in the eye. Juanita was sure that if they had been the same sex, they would have been the best of friends. In many ways, Rita exuded the same strength in Canada that Rodriguez had once possessed in Guatemala.

One day Rita saw Juanita's paintings of the children. Juanita spoke of how she longed to get back to this artwork but could never find the time, or get the approval of her husband. Rita filed these things away in the back of her mind.

In the middle of a hot August afternoon, Rita came over to visit Juanita, with a spare ticket in her hand for the women's music festival. She announced to Rodriguez that his wife would come with her to the festival, and that it was important for Juanita to be inspired by the art of others. There would be artists at the festival. As she spoke, Rita's eyes caressed the paintings of Juanita's children, where they hung in the living room above the television. She left the ticket in Juanita's hand and said she would be back on Sunday, early, to pick up her friend.

"This one thing I will do," Juanita told Rodriguez, and herself, before either his voice or her misgivings could protest. When Rita came on Sunday morning, Juanita was ready and waiting outside.

At the festival, the artwork on display was beautiful. But, for Juanita, the best event of the day was a black woman singing her dub poetry. Her name was Lillian Allen, and she read/sang about having a baby, her own little girl:

An this little girl wouldn't come a minute before she ready, fiborn.
An mi labour.
An mi labour.
An mi labour.
An mi push an mi push an mi push ...

In her mind, Juanita could clearly see that little baby girl ride down her mother's birth canal. This was something she knew about.

At the end of the performance, Juanita ran up to the poet and offered, "Ms. Allen, if you have another baby ever, I will be honoured to sit as your midwife, sf?"

Lillian Allen rolled back her head, laughed, and said, "A-haaaa. Allrighhht, sister."

That night when Juanita got home, she watched Rodriguez sleeping and then she watched her sleeping children. She pulled out her paints from the corner of the balcony porch, and she painted out her feelings of that day. The painting became an imaginary depiction of Lillian Allen's baby, and a celebration of birth.

From that time on, Juanita returned to her easel. Over the following days and months, she searched her memory and recreated many of the paintings her father had made her burn, and the paintings she had thrown away when she became Rodriguez' wife and they went into the jungle as revolutionaries. Rodriguez, who on the day that she went to the festival had stopped talking with Juanita unless he absolutely had to, saw that she was not going to stop. Eventually he began communicating with her again.

Together, Juanita and Rodriguez decided to have one more baby before finishing that part of their lives for good. And that baby was part of Juanita's first and only self-portrait, as she watched in the mirror while he emerged from her body.

TARA

A letter from Juanita comes the next morning just before noon. I have just awakened, after writing late into the night. I decide to go down to the beach and read the letter there. I stuff it into my straw bag along with a beach towel, my bathing suit and suntan lotion.

Outside it is sunny. The birds are singing. I can smell the red camellias and see them bursting out through the green vines on the buildings and telephone poles. I walk slowly. I need a rest after working so hard at my writing over the last while.

I change into my navy-blue bathing suit in the bath house. I get out onto the beach and spread my towel over the mocha-coloured sand. I lay down on my stomach, squirm a bit to even out the bumpy sand under my torso and tear open Juanita's letter.

My Dear Friend,

Rita apologizes for the postcard. She has been very busy teaching more sessional courses than she should.

But we want you to know that by being good and kind enough to work on everyone else's story, you may be neglecting to get your own down. Or perhaps you are "avoiding" as Rita says.

It does not matter enough to break up friendships. I am honoured you are working on my story.

I hope you will come back home. We do need you to share your writing skills. A group of women from Latin America (mostly refugees) have come to Rita and me with the idea of putting their stories together in a book. We have listened to their stories now, here and there, over a few days. We are starting to realize what you realize: how their difficulties right now could

*be lessened and how other Canadians would surely be more
tolerant if they knew these women's stories.*

*We are applying for a grant and they say we have a good
chance of getting it. Will you return to work with these women?
Please let me know soon. They want to begin writing their stories
now that they have come up with the idea. Also ...*

Something is stinging my legs.

Pebbles are hitting them.

I look up. Peering over the stone fence between the beach and
a path to some ritzy hotels further down is a handsome young
man with a head of thick, black curls.

"Bad girl," he leers at me, then says something in Greek
which, by the tone of his voice, must mean "whore" or something equally derogatory.

I am a woman alone, laying on the beach, so I am assumed
to be a whore, a bad girl.

Anger centres in my stomach. Still, I put my head back down
and close my eyes. I want him to go away. I do not want to have
the trouble of a confrontation. I just want to relax.

He throws two more pebbles. They sting.

My anger forces its way up to my mouth like heartburn. I
retch it out. "You fucking asshole," I scream and spring to my
feet. "Leave me alone you fucking little creep."

Right before my eyes, the young man turns into a boy. First,
he pouts, but as I continue to yell, he becomes frightened. People
at the outdoor cafe across the path are staring. Passing tourists
gawk with their mouths hanging open. "Take it easy lady," says
one man, whose face is burned beet-red. "It's not such a big
deal."

I don't care. I have to vent my rage. "Just fuck right off," I
yell at the boy. Now his cheeks burn red. He turns and runs.

My anger chokes me. Fighting back the tears, I shove stuff
back into my straw bag.

I rush over to the road and along the boardwalk to another
part of the hill.

I come to a pasture. It remains, even though hotel develop-
ments rise ominously around it. I see a shepherd with his flock

of brown sheep and goats. They munch slowly, move slowly, munch some more grass. The shepherd is old and bent over. I see he wears a brown wool sweater, knitted, I guess, from his own sheep's wool. There are purple and yellow and white wildflowers scattered all over the field.

I do not feel violent anymore. The feeling is buried deep and hard inside me still, but it no longer itches on the surface.

I need to write now. Writing is a friend. She will comfort.

TARA'S STORY

(a fragment)

At the typewriter the first thing that seeps out of me is this:

This spring I went down to a cabin on Lake Winnipeg with a bunch of women friends and we cried aloud each time we spotted a yellow ladyslipper in the underbrush, celebrated its beauty with a chant.

When I was a kid, a teeny-bopper, I knew this girl, a young woman. We were friends. She'd open her legs to any guy. Lucky them, but they were too out of it to know it. She told me once there was nothing more beautiful than making love. Around the same time she told me she had gone on the pill 'cause she wanted to be a bad girl that summer. It's just like that feminist academic said, my friend was seeing herself half like the guys saw her when they gang-banged her in the back seat of one of their Daddy's cars. The other half, the part about beautiful love, was her own half—talking, feeling.

You know I could still weep for her even now.

Guys down by the lake used to ride their dirt bikes over yellow ladyslippers, when I was a kid. They ripped through tree branches. Crushed out, choked off, anything they sort of thought might be beautiful. Sort of thought, I say, 'cause I don't know if they ever knew just what beauty was. They wouldn't know it if they were fucking it.

When I desire a man for the beauty sparking between us, just itching to be stroked and licked and rubbed in circles growing bigger and further apart like the ripples left by a small grey pebble tossed into a cool, still lake and turning over and over and over ...

On those days when I try to hide these feelings 'cause I know guys think it's bad for women to want to open their legs up and—who knows?—I could even be gang-banged for it.

On those days when I can't understand for the life of me what's wrong with a woman wanting to make beauty with someone and just going ahead and doing it.

On those days I could still weep.

Still, it's not quite me—although it is me, in the sense that I was friends with this woman, was close to her when these things happened, lived in the community where these things happened.

I am getting closer.

I sleep.

I do not dream.

I am ten years old. As I go down the steps that lead to the cloakroom in the school basement it is dark as usual. I have delayed as long as I possibly can and I know my mother will be very angry with me if I'm late, so I force myself to go down.

It is possible that he might not be there today. I can always hope. I always do hope.

He moves out from underneath the stairwell. He is tall, twice my height. And big, with muscular arms. He is dirty. He smells.

He blocks my path when I get to the bottom of the stairs. I move to one side hoping to get around him. He moves over in front of me.

It becomes like a dance: I shuffle one way, he moves in front of me; I move the other way, he shuffles in front of me.

Someone is coming at the top of the stairs. He yanks my breasts, pulls one with each of his hands. I feel the pain of being torn there. "Whore," he whispers.

"Tara, pull back your shoulders," my father tells me jovially. "Don't go around humped over all the time. Are you scared of getting a chest?"

He grabs between my legs, through my pants, pulls the skin and pubic hair away from the bone underneath.

The hurt is sharp. "Whore," he whispers.

"Oh, Tara, they were just poking between your legs," my mother says. "Don't be so silly. It's nothing."

Until spring when I no longer have to wear a parka, this happens to me every morning. Soon, I stop moving away because he does it faster then. It's over with faster then.

I am eleven years old. I have chicken pox. My mother leaves me with my aunt and uncle because she has some kind of business to take care of. My aunt goes out for a few minutes and my uncle tells me to come downstairs.

"Come on, come on," he urges. He is being very friendly. His cheeks are already red from drinking whisky even though it's still morning. His lips pull back away from his false teeth in a grin like a caricature.

Next I remember I am backing up the stairs, away from my uncle masturbating in front of me in the basement.

At the head of the stairs, my aunt confronts me. "What were you doing down there? Why did you go down there?"

I am confused. I seem to have done something wrong but I don't know what.

TARA

I stop writing. There is more but I need a break. I cannot tell everything. Not yet. I realize I do not even remember everything, not yet.

I get my swim things and head for the sea.

I swim and, although I am usually a weak swimmer, my strokes today are surprisingly strong.

I get out and lay down on my towel. The sun is so warm. It massages my body and I feel drowsy.

The dream has changed so much now. There is yellow sunshine and green fields, and green where the fire has been. A tree is growing in the middle of the circle.

I walk into the circle and my voice rings out loud and clear. The other four listen intently. More people stand and listen in the surrounding fields.

When I can speak no more, other voices fill the air.

I move out of the inner circle and Juanita moves into it. I know that it is her turn to speak.

When I wake, the sun is going down over the harbour and behind the fort. I get up, put a large tee-shirt over my bathing suit and put my things back into the straw bag. I head towards the travel agency down by the harbour cafés. It's time to go home.

TANYA LESTER is a former Administrative Coordinator of the Manitoba Action Committee on the Status of Women. Her stories, reviews and articles have been widely published and she has worked as an editor and playwright. She works for the Popular Theatre Alliance of Manitoba and teaches writing for Age & Opportunity with the University of Winnipeg Continuing Education Program. She has previously published a collection of short stories called Dreams and Tricksters (1985). She lives in Winnipeg with her son Luke.

THE BEST OF *gynergy books*

■ **A House Not Her Own: Stories from Beirut,**
Emily Nasrallah. In seventeen powerful and poetic stories, this internationally acclaimed Lebanese author and feminist writes about what she knows only too well: war and the civilians who live within the bombed-out shell of Beirut, who try to recreate a past through memories, even as the landmarks and monuments of that past are destroyed.
ISBN 0-921881-19-3 $ 12.95

■ **By Word of Mouth: Lesbians write the erotic,**
Lee Fleming (ed.). A bedside book of short fiction and poetry by thirty-one lesbian writers.
ISBN 0-921881-06-1 $ 10.95 / $ 12.95 US

■ **Don't: A Woman's Word**, *Elly Danica*. The best-selling account of incest and recovery, both horrifying and hauntingly beautiful in its eventual triumph over the past.
ISBN 0-921881-05-3 $ 8.95 (US rights held by Cleis Press)

■ **Each Small Step: Breaking the chains of abuse and addiction,** *Marilyn MacKinnon (ed.).* This groundbreaking anthology contains narratives by women recovering from the traumas of childhood sexual abuse and alcohol and chemical dependency.
ISBN 0-921881-17-7 $ 10.95

■ **The Montreal Massacre,** *Marie Chalouh and Louise Malette (eds.).* Feminist letters, essays and poems examine the misogyny inherent in the mass murder of fourteen women at École Polytechnique in Montreal, Quebec on December 6, 1989.
ISBN 0-921881-14-2 $ 12.95

■ **Sous la langue / Under Tongue,** *Nicole Brossard.* "Brossard's language rolls under tongue, over tongue, around and around inside the body. Sensual. Erotic." *(f.) Lip*
ISBN 0-921881-00-2 $ 15.00

■ **Tide Lines: Stories of change by lesbians,** *Lee Fleming (ed.).* These diverse stories explore the many faces of change— instantaneous, over-a-lifetime, subtle or cataclysmic.
ISBN 0-921881-15-0 $ 10.95

gynergy books can be found in quality bookstores, or individual orders can be sent, prepaid, to: *gynergy books,* P.O. Box 2023, Charlottetown, PEI, Canada, C1A 7N7. Please add postage and handling ($1.50 for the first book and 75 cents for each additional book) to your order. Canadian residents add 7% GST to the total amount. GST registration number R104383120.